The Fisher King

A NOVEL

Paule Marshall

Scribner

NEW YORK   LONDON   TORONTO   SYDNEY   SINGAPORE

SCRIBNER
1230 Avenue of the Americas
New York, NY 10020

Designed by Brooke Koven

Set in New Caledonia

Manufactured in the United States of America

Marshall, Paule.
The fisher king: a novel/Paule Marshall.

ISBN 0-684-87283-8

For the memory of

my cousin, Sonny Clement, baritone sax

Earl Griffith, vibes

Ernie Henry, alto sax

And especially for

Neats and Lesley

The author wishes to express her gratitude to the MacArthur Foundation for its endorsement and support.

A special praisesong of thanks to my friend, Mme Christina Davis of Paris, for her invaluable assistance.

Thanks also to Patrick Salès and Helen Ellis.

"You got some of all of us in you, dontcha? What you gonna do with all that Colored from all over creation you got in you? Better be somethin' good."
—Florence Varina McCullum-Jones

The
Fisher King

1

*"Had the brass-face to come round me
playing the Sodom and Gomorrah music!"*

The old woman they said was his great-grandmother stood eyeing him from behind the locked iron gate to the basement of her house. She had ordered that he be brought to see her as soon as he arrived, if not the same day, then the one following. In either case, he was to visit her first, she'd said, before any of the other relatives, and certainly before "the old-miss-young" across the street at No. 258 Macon. And the visit was to last a full hour. She had insisted on that also.

Yet minutes had passed and she had made no move to open the gate and let him in. Nor had she spoken as yet, even though Hattie who had brought him over for the visit and was standing waiting behind him had politely greeted the woman and introduced him when she answered the bell.

"Hello, Mrs. Payne, it's Hattie," she'd said. "Hattie Carmichael? You might not recognize me it's been so long, so many years . . . And this is Sonny. His name's Sonny."

Not a word. Her rheumy, clouded-over eyes immediately latching onto his face, the woman hadn't said a word. Nor had she so much as glanced at Hattie.

He waited, puzzled, Hattie behind him, her height and bulk shielding him from the wind that had followed them into the bare front yard of the house. A late March wind that was behaving as if it were still the depths of winter. On the way over, it had buffeted them past the houses lining either side of the long street. They were row houses the like of which he had never seen before, all of them four stories tall under lowering, beetle-browed cornices, all of them hewn out of a dark, somber reddish-brown stone, and all with high stoops of a dozen or more steps slanting sharply down from the second story to the yard. Because of the raised, high-stepping stoops, the brown uniform houses made him think of an army goosestepping toward an enemy that was a mirror image of itself across the street.

Then there was the heavy wrought-iron basement gate under the side of each stoop, identical to the one rearing up just inches from his face. A dungeon gate with arrowhead bars like spears. He liked it. Liked also the marching houses. Castles. Something about them reminded him of the castles and fortresses he was good at drawing.

The woman he'd been told was his great-grandmother continued her silent scrutiny of him. For his part, he had already noted as much of her as he cared to, from the battered old-lady hat on top of her uncombed hair down to the none-too-clean housedress to be glimpsed under a long, shapeless cardigan that was as heavy as a coat hanging on her tall bony frame.

The few buttons left on the sweater were all in the wrong holes and there were food stains on it as well as on the dress.

Like a two-year-old, he thought, who didn't know how to dress or feed itself good.

Worse, there was her hand. You're not to stare Hattie was always admonishing him. This time he couldn't help it. There was nothing wrong with the woman's right hand. That was okay. But behind the tall bars of the gate, her left hand kept up a trembly dance at her side.

Did he really want someone like her for a relative?

"Is something wrong, Mrs. Payne?" Hattie's voice at his back. "Have you changed your mind? Should I maybe bring him back another day?"

A cut-eye. The woman finally acknowledged Hattie's presence with a single venomous cut-eye and returned her gaze to his face.

It came to Sonny then: the gate wouldn't open, the visit would not take place, so long as Hattie stood drawn up behind him as if waiting to barge into the house the moment he was admitted. She was not, it had been agreed, to be part of the visit. The man who had met them at the airport two days ago and driven them in his big, fast car to this strange place called Brooklyn—his great-uncle Edgar the man had called himself—had prevailed upon Hattie to let him visit the woman alone.

That's another thing the great-grandmother woman had insisted on. He was to be alone with her. Not even the man, who was her son, was to be present.

"You don't mind, do you?" the man had asked him. "A big boy like you."

"No," he had lied.

"I warn you, she's old and acts a little odd at times, but you're not to let it bother you. After all, she's family and blood."

"There're all kinds of family and blood's got nothing to do with it!" Hattie.

She had sounded to Sonny as if ready to take him and herself right back home on the plane that had brought them.

The man had hastily agreed with her.

Now she was saying to the woman, and she was no longer being polite, "All right, Mrs. Payne, I get the message. I'm leaving. But I'll be back for him in an hour, if not before. He's to meet his other great-grandmother this morning too, y'know. She's got as much right to him as anybody else around here!"

Then, bending down to hug him from behind, Hattie repeated the instructions she'd given him earlier: if there was a problem or he didn't like it or if anything happened to upset or frighten him he was to phone her and she'd come get him right away.

To prevent the woman from understanding, she had switched from English to French. Or what with Hattie passed for French. Terrible. Sonny hadn't realized just how terrible was the scrambled, make-do French she spoke until he started school.

Did he have the slip of paper with the number where they were staying in his pocket?

"*Oui,*" he said; and deeply offended by the cutting look she'd been dealt, Hattie, his fathermothersisterbrother and all the "kin" he'd ever known, was gone.

The moment she turned out of the yard, the woman unlocked the dungeon gate.

It took her a while because of the trembly hand.

That done, she spoke for the first time. "Come out the cold, nuh!"

       ✻   ✻   ✻

Inside, fearful but curious, he followed her down a long dim hallway that wasn't much warmer than outside. And that had a smell. The basement or ground floor of the woman's house had a dank, musty, stale-kitchen smell and there was so little light that for all his curiosity he couldn't see much of anything except shadows, large, unwelcoming shadows observing him on either side.

He kept close on the woman's heels.

As if to make up for the time lost waiting for Hattie to leave, she was moving at a stiff but urgent shuffle. Midway down the hall, a walled-in staircase loomed up to their right and, without bothering to check on him behind her, she started up the steps.

She climbed, one halting baby step at a time, while he hung back at the bottom, unable to see where to place his foot the darkness on the walled-in stairs was so dense.

"Come 'long, nuh!"

He scrambled blindly up. Yelling at him! Annoyed, he would've sneaked a look under her dress to get back at her had there been any light. It was wrong, but he would have done it anyway.

Upstairs, on the second floor, another long hall led back toward the front of the house. There was somewhat more light here, although it only served to reveal a shameful state of neglect and dirt everywhere. Cracked and peeling walls. Large turds of dust like tumbleweed. Overhead, the rusted pipes of a defunct sprinkler system lined what had once been a beautiful coffered ceiling. Underfoot, the filthy hall runner was worn clear through to the floorboards down its center.

He would tell Hattie on her: that she had yelled at him and that she kept her house no better than she kept herself.

Near the front of the hall, she came to a halt at the foot

of a wide staircase leading to the two upper floors of the house. Then, abruptly: "Turn off the lights and the blasted radios up there!" The woman suddenly shouting like a drill sergeant up the dark and silent stairs. "You think I own Con Edison? Damn roomers! You's more trouble than profit!"

Before he could see the lights or hear the radios for himself, he was bounding after her over to an elaborately carved double door on their left. As was true of all the woodwork in the hall, the joined doors had clearly not been polished in years; nevertheless they were still handsome, stately, tall, reaching almost to the high ceiling, the kind of doors he'd seen only in a church.

These, the woman opened. Or rather, she made them disappear. With what seemed to him an abracadabra motion of her hands—including the shaky one—on the handles, she sent both halves of the great door rumbling out of sight.

Magic. True, he saw the metal track in the floor and the long slender pockets in either wall, yet it nonetheless seemed like something magical she alone had done.

He was suddenly less annoyed with her.

Through the wide doorway, the old woman ushered Sonny into a shuttered, airless living room filled to overflow with an assortment of shabby, mismatched furniture, none of it arranged in any order. A living room that had originally been a formal Victorian front parlor, although now it looked like a dark, dusty warehouse or a secondhand furniture store that hadn't had a sale in years.

Moving with even greater urgency, she led him through the clutter over to an old upright piano that had an unusually high front.

Out of everything in the room the piano alone stood dusted and polished.

There she stopped. "Take off yuh coat, nuh."

His new coat. Hattie had bought it for him only days ago with money from the check sent her by the man who had met them at the airport. After threatening for weeks to tear up both the check and the letter that had accompanied it and toss the pieces like so much *poubelle,* garbage, into the Seine, she had finally changed her mind and used the money to outfit him in everything new from head to toe.

"No need for you to go there looking like a pauper," she'd said.

He handed over the coat as well as his hat and gloves to the woman, who then pointed to his shoes, new also. He was to remove them too.

Why? He started to ask why only to see her stiffen. About to yell at him again.

He did as ordered.

The shoes off, she waved him up on the piano bench. He was not to sit though. Another wave directed him to stand. And when he did, when he stood up on the bench in his socks, he found himself face-to-face on top of the piano with a large, framed photograph of a boy more or less his age. A primly posed, unsmiling boy a lesser shade of brownish-black than himself and all dressed up in an old-timey suit and high-topped shoes, his hair neatly parted on one side, his hands neatly clasped in his lap.

The boy in the photograph appeared to be seated at the same piano, his back to it, and on the stand behind lay a music book. Through the sepia cast of the picture, a large *B* could be seen on the music book's cover, followed by an *A*, a *C*, and ending with *H*.

The woman stood quietly, almost reverently, examining the photograph with him, until all of a sudden, without warning, she swung angrily away from it and was shouting again—this time up at the cobwebbed ceiling—"Had the brass-face to come round me playing the Sodom and Gomorrah music!"

Then, her voice normal again: "Sit," she said.

He quickly dropped down on the bench and she uncovered the keyboard.

" I don't know how to play," he said.

She ignored this and reaching around him from behind opened the panels in the piano's high front. To his astonishment, there inside the piano, in its innards, stood a long roll of white paper, paper whiter and cleaner than anything he had seen so far in the house. Instead of the usual cat's cradle of strings and the little felt-tipped hammers that even he knew was what made the music when you struck the keys, there was something that looked like a giant roll of *papier hygiénique*. What was toilet paper doing inside a piano? All the more puzzling, someone had taken a razor blade and made any number of little cuts and nicks all over it.

Before he could find his tongue, more magic: the giant roll of white paper began to move. The woman pressed a switch to the left of the keyboard and the paper began moving. In the same instant, keys to the left and right of where he sat, the yellowed ivory ones as well as the faded black keys, began moving at random, sinking down and then rising, rapidly sinking and rising entirely on their own. And music, music as tall and stately and ecclesiastic as the doors the woman had made vanish, came pouring forth.

Sonny looked up at her dumbstruck and she touched him. Bending over him, enveloping him in what Hattie would have called a B.O. smell mixed together with the damp mustiness of her basement, she took his hands in both of hers.

The woman's fluttering left hand closing around his. The feel of it! Scared, repelled, he tried pulling away.

"Hold still!"

Maintaining her grip, she then did two things that in the next few minutes would make him forget for the time being the scary feel of her hand. First, she slowly spread his fingers and arched them slightly. This done, she then began guiding his hands to where the keys left and right were sinking down, trying to reach them and place his fingers on as many of them as possible in the fraction of a second before they rose again.

For the longest time she repeatedly steered his hands back and forth across the keyboard, showing him how the game was played, while the huge sheet of paper with its hieroglyphics of cuts and nicks scrolled majestically down before his eyes, and the music soared.

Finally she released his hands, stood up from over him, said, "All right now, you's to play till I say stop," and went and sat down nearby.

He was suddenly on his own. At first, he missed all of the keys. They would fall and rise before he even came close. He wasn't fast enough, alert enough, and his fingers were too short. It was a frustrating scramble that made him want to bring his fist like a sledgehammer down on the keyboard or throw himself on the floor and kick and rage as if he were a baby again. Until gradually, ever so slowly as he kept at it, his eyes grew more alert to the slightest movement on either side of him and his fingers became faster in tracking his eyes to the spot. Eventually he was reaching some of the keys just as they began to descend and pressing them down completely. He was the one causing them to sink before they quickly rose again. It was all his doing! So that while it remained a game, he convinced himself that he was actually playing. He, Sonny Carmichael Payne, was the one creating the lofty music and not just some oversize roll of *papier hygiénique.*

As for the keys he missed, which was most of them, he was enjoying himself too much to care.

What did the woman think of his playing? He paused to look over at her. She was seated in a sagging, overstuffed armchair that looked as if a generation of feral cats had used its padded legs as a scratching post, the upholstery in shreds. Under her hat which she hadn't taken off (nor had she removed the sweater that was as heavy as a coat), her eyes were closed. Had she nodded off? Hattie did that sometimes. He caught, though, the hint of a smile. The forbidding woman smiling? Her right hand clamped down hard on its ungovernable twin to keep it quiet in her lap, she was listening to the music with what he could swear was the trace of a smile on her aged, fallen face.

Perhaps he might get to like her a little, he thought. Her magic. Her special piano. Her games. All that might help him to overlook not only the slovenly state of both her and her house, but her habit of shouting at persons unseen, as well as at him. He might also get used to the way she talked. Her English was different from Hattie's.

As for that hand of hers . . . he might even get used to that. After all, look at his *nounou,* his sitter, old Madame Molineaux, who minded him the nights that Hattie worked. Didn't she have a funny thing she did with her head? For as long as he could remember, Madame Molineaux's ancient head had always kept up a little nervous side-to-side motion she couldn't help. Her head going side to side like the pendulum of an old-fashioned clock. Because of it, she always appeared to be saying *non, non, non* to everything, *non, non, non* even when she meant *oui.*

He hardly noticed it anymore he was so used to it.

Nor was Madame Molineaux all that clean. Wasn't Hattie always complaining that the way she kept her apartment, which was next door to theirs, was enough to turn your stomach?

He turned back to the dancing keyboard. This time, to help him out and to make the game more fun, he reached up to the top of the piano. He grew his arm to twice its length and easily hauled down the prim, old-timey boy in the picture to sit beside him on the bench. He unclasped the neatly folded hands, crooked the fingers slightly as the woman had done with his, and after quickly showing him what to do, put him to work chasing down the keys to the right of the keyboard.

He would concentrate on those to the left.

Wait'll he told Hattie he had learned to play the piano on his very first try!

2

The Three R's Housing Group of Central Brooklyn
Reclamation. Restoration. Rebirth.
207 Reid Avenue
Brooklyn, New York 11233

Edgar DeC. Payne, Director

February 6, 1984

Ms. Hattie Carmichael
130, rue Sauffroy
75017 Paris, France

Dear Hattie Carmichael:

It's been so many years, I feel I must address you in this somewhat formal manner. Truthfully, though, I still remember you and think of you as simply Hattie "from around the block," just as all of us who grew up on Macon Street were simply "from around the block" back in the old days.

In any case, after much effort I recently obtained the above address for you and decided to write concerning a matter which I'm sure you will find of interest. In two months' time, on Friday, April 6th to be exact, there's to be a memorial concert in honor of my brother. That date, as you know, marks the fifteenth anniversary of his tragic death. The event will be held on home ground; that is, right here in Brooklyn, and it is to be a major tribute to him and to his music, something you will agree is long overdue.

You will also agree, I hope, that it is important, indeed imperative, that you attend. I know that like my brother and Cherisse, you vowed never to set eyes on these United States again, and you have kept that vow over the years. This letter is to ask that you make an exception just this once. The concert would not be the same without you. After all, you were the one closest to my brother's work from the beginning; and you, more than anyone else, including the critics, understood what he was attempting to do and say with his music. So how can you not be present?

As for the concert, everything is being done to ensure its success. It's to be held at Putnam Royal where, as you know better than I, my brother first made his name. I should add that the Royal is no longer the run-down barn of a place you remember. The local housing and development group I head up bought the building last year and we have practically restored it to the grand old hall it was originally. You'll be pleased at the transformation. The concert will not only memorialize my brother, it will inaugurate a restored, reborn Putnam Royal. It will be an historic occasion on a number of counts in other words, all the more reason for you to be there.

Naturally, we would ask that you bring Sonny with you. He should be present at this tribute to his grandfather. It would also give those of us on this side of the Atlantic a chance to meet him, as well as to thank you personally for having rescued him. From what we've learned of his mother's behavior, who knows what would have become of him had it not been for you. Of course, we miss not having news of him from time to time. I can't tell you how it pains us that you have chosen to continue the silence and estrangement that were true when my brother and Cherisse were alive.

That aside, please bring him if only for the sake of his great-grandmothers. They are both close to ninety and this might be their only chance to see him. I should add that those two still don't have a kind word to say about each other. Perhaps the sight of their great-grand will help them to forgive and forget, if only to a degree. At any rate, they're both eager to meet him.

In fact, it would be ideal if you could manage to come a few weeks before the concert so that Sonny could visit around. My two grandchildren can't wait to get a look at their Parisian second cousin. My own hopes are such that I've taken the liberty of arranging for a pair of tickets for you at Air France. You are to choose the dates you wish to travel. Also, the enclosed check is to cover any expenses you might have in preparing for the trip. You're to let me know if more is needed.

Again, dear Hattie Carmichael, do agree to come. Your visit will mean so much to all of us here. Your presence at the concert, where you and Sonny will of course be honored guests, will make this celebration and commemoration of my brother's life and genius complete in every respect.

Please let me hear from you soon.

Sincerely,

Edgar

"From around the block."

3

"Been holding in too much too long!"

"**I** learned to play her piano."

Hattie abruptly stopped in the middle of the sidewalk, folded her arms across her chest, and waited for him to explain himself.

"I did! I'm not making it up." Why did she always think he was making things up! "She showed me how and I was playing."

"Just like that, eh?"

"*Oui!* It was this special piano . . ." He started to describe it, switching to French because the words came easier. He didn't get far before Hattie laughed and resumed walking.

"Her old player piano. I forgot about that thing," she said. "It's a wonder it still works."

"Well it does and I was playing it."

"Pretend-play, you mean."

"*Non!* She showed me how and . . ."

"Okay, okay, if you say so. So what else did the two of you do?"

He had decided even before Hattie came for him that he wasn't going to tell on the woman after all. All the things that were wrong with her and her house he would keep to himself. So he simply said, "Nothing. I just practiced my playing."

Over the past hour the wind had abated somewhat, the cold had lessened its grip, and the sun, hidden up to now, was struggling to break through clouds that were the color of pewter. As it was midmorning, few people aside from themselves were to be seen on the street and even fewer cars.

Their destination, No. 258 Macon, was on the opposite side of the street and closer to the corner where they had to cross. It would turn out to be the best house on the block. Because while all the old high-stoop, martial-looking brownstones were alike, fashioned from the same mold, they differed widely in condition and upkeep. A number were well kept, but far too many were as neglected-looking as inside the house Sonny had just left. Some of these were being renovated, it was true. Scaffolds were up and the two of them passed men wearing hard hats who were busy working despite the cold, the noisy chorus of their hammers and other tools dominating the midmorning quiet. But more often than not, the renovations were taking place right next to a near-ruin that was completely boarded up, its windows filled in with cinder blocks, a condemned notice from the city posted on the door, and the front yard choked with litter and dried weeds that were taller than Sonny.

Not so No. 258. It was what all the houses on Macon Street must have looked like when the reddish-brown sandstone with which they were built was first quarried. Old as it was, it looked new. As they entered the front gate, Sonny's awed gaze took in the stained-glass fanlight above the carved and polished double-leaf door at the top of the stoop and the fringed and scalloped shades at the lofty windows. A tree. A tree stood in the meticulous yard, a large tree in full leaf as if it were the height of summer, and with a shiny bronze plaque on its trunk.

A plaque on a tree? What did it say?

He was about to ask if he could go over and see if he could read what it said when Hattie, her hand suddenly tense around his, started up the stoop.

"She said for us to come up to the parlor floor."

"What's that?"

"It's what they call the second floor in these old houses."

"What's her name again?"

She had told him earlier, but it was too long a name to remember.

"Mrs. Florence Varina McCullum-Jones, even though she hardly ever used the Jones part as I remember."

Hattie's voice was also tense.

No sooner had she rung the bell at the top of the stoop than one half of the great door opened and they were being warmly greeted by a large, wide-hipped woman in a parlor-maid's frilly little white apron and cap.

"Lord, Mis' McCullum been up and dressed and waiting on you since early this morning," she said, beaming down on him as she ushered them into the vestibule. The vestibule had a beautiful inlaid marble floor and oak wainscoting that came up to Sonny's shoulders. After taking their coats, the maid opened another door, this one paneled in beveled glass, and there beyond this inner door, inside the formal parlor floor hall, stood a small, bent, almost doll-like old woman with bobbed, russet-colored hair, pearl earrings, a pearl choker with enough strands to cover her entire neck, and, above the choker, a deeply lined face that was as carefully made up as a cover girl's.

To receive him, she was wearing a brightly patterned at-home gown. What looked like a pair of high-heeled mules peeked out from under the hem.

"My baby's grandbaby!"

The dressed-up woman gathered him to her with a tearful cry. Her arms were not much longer than his.

He right away liked her smell. It made him think of Hattie's when she finished her toilette before leaving for work at the Club Violette in the evenings. The combined drift through the apartment of her scented soap, creams, lotions, dusting powder, and cologne was an aura that lingered long after she kissed him and left for the night and Madame Molineaux took over.

The woman they said was also his great-grandmother continued to embrace him tearfully. Until, finally collecting herself, she released him and turned to Hattie. Speaking in a rush, her voice strangely tight and her eyes not quite meeting Hattie's, she thanked her for taking him and raising him as her own (God was going to reward her) and for bringing him to visit her at last (her prayers had been answered), nobody knew how many times she had wanted to take a plane old as she was and fly over to Paris, France, to see him for herself, although she wouldn't have known where to find him, seeing as there had been no return address on the letter—the one letter!—informing her of his birth, but never mind, all that was water under the bridge, it didn't matter anymore, her baby's grandbaby was here.

The woman saying all this in the rushed, tight voice and without really looking at Hattie. Then, after introducing the large maid whose name was Dora, she led them into her living room.

"Now don't go getting yourself all excited, Mis' McCullum. You know it's no good for you," Dora called after her.

The woman fanned her down.

The room they entered put to shame the one he'd just left. It was the way, he thought, a room in a *palais royal* back home might look. Chandeliers. Not one but two crystal chandeliers hung at either end of the high, long, molded ceiling. Large, gilt-framed mirrors were everywhere, one of them reaching like a waterfall from the high ceiling to the floor. He saw himself reflected in his new clothes wherever he looked. A huge fireplace repeated the marble in the vestibule. And then there was the elegant, old-timey furniture arranged over the gleaming floor as if poised, breath held, waiting to begin a stately dance to the music he'd just been playing.

It was the kind of room where someone like himself, a kid, was to go and sit hands clasped in his lap and dare not touch anything.

Hattie appeared equally impressed.

Holding on to him, the woman seated herself on a camel-back sofa that sat like a throne at the front of the room, facing everything there. Behind it, a triptych of windows looked down on her perfect yard and the tree in summer leaf.

She drew him to her knees, tilted his head toward the light. "Now lemme get a good look at you. See who-all you take after."

Being scrutinized for a second time. But where the face of the great-grandmother woman across the street had been unreadable behind her basement gate, not so with this one. It wasn't long before a frown further deepened the lines already etched deep in her face. Clearly, there was much about him, certain features, that didn't please her.

For a time she tried erasing them, it seemed, by the sheer force of her gaze. When that failed, she became impatient and pulling herself up purposefully, she took his face between her warped little hands, placed her thumbs at the outer corners of his eyes and, without hurting him, stretched them slightly upward.

A triumphant cry: "He's got the McCullum eyes! There's no getting around the fact those old W.I.s across the street put their mark on him, poor baby, but he's got the McCullum eyes, one thing, and that's what counts!"

She continued her examination. At one point, she swiped his cheek with the tip of her finger, as if expecting the color there to come off like soot. She herself, he'd already noted, was the tawny yellow-brown of the lions in the zoo in the Bois de Vincennes.

"Who's the daddy?" Holding up the finger to Hattie who had taken a seat some distance from them. "African?"

Hattie, who hadn't said a word as yet, simply nodded.

Dismay for a moment, followed by a philosophical sigh, and then the woman was smiling at him. "You got some of all of us in you, dontcha? What you gonna do with all that Colored from all over creation you got in you? Better be somethin' good."

He didn't understand, so he shrugged. She immediately mimicked him, and in such an outlandish way, wriggling her little bent, bony shoulders and trying to raise them as high as the pearl earrings, that he couldn't help but laugh.

The laugh earned him another fragrant hug.

"Oh, I'm so happy to see my baby's grandbaby! Didn't I pray each night for this day! And just look at how you got all dressed to meet your great-grandma! A real little gentle-man from Paris, France!"

Suddenly: "Know what? Know what I'm gonna do? I'm gonna show you off to the world! Oh yes I am! And starting this very Thursday at my tour guide talk.

"I'm still working for the Landmarks Conservancy people, you know." This to Hattie. "I'm still giving my tour guide talks."

"Oh. I thought you would've retired long ago." Hattie's voice was as tight as the woman's earlier.

"The Conservancy people won't let me! They won't hear of me retiring. Why? 'Cause mine's the best stop of the tour, that's why!" A proud cry. "Has been for close to forty years! Every group they bring here just loves the talk I give. Those old tours would be nothing without the stop at Two fifty-eight Macon Street. The Conservancy people know that. That's why they've always treated me special . . ."

For one, maintaining the house for her, she said. Inside and out. For another, caring for the tree in the yard her father had planted close to a hundred years ago. They had also helped her find nice, quiet, hardworking tenants for the two upper floors of the house. And had found Dora (a godsend!) to take care of her and seen to it the City paid her salary. All she did was buy her the pretty little aprons and caps. Yes, the Conservancy people treated her special.

"They know which side their bread is buttered on. Don't think they don't . . ."

The woman talking talking talking, her nonstop voice shaking her slight frame like the March wind outdoors.

"You didn't know that your great-grandma was a working girl, did you?"

He shook his head no.

"Well, she is. People from all over come and pay good money to hear me talk about that tree outside, this house, and the McCullums. Which means you too"—she pinched the cheek she had swiped minutes ago—"seeing as you're one of us. Partly anyways . . ."

Suddenly, like a citywide power failure, all her brightness and enthusiasm died, her dark, unhappy frown returned, and tears—angry ones this time—welled up.

She sat him down next to her on the sofa so that she could have an unobstructed view of Hattie.

"Why'd you have to go name him after that man?"

She was looking at her head-on now.

Hattie didn't answer immediately. Instead, acting as if she hadn't heard, she began fussing with her skirt which lay pooled around her on the parquet floor. Hattie was wearing her standard outfit, a sweeping ankle-length skirt and a matching loose-fitting tunic with a high neck and great bat-winged dolman sleeves. It was the way she dressed all the time, the ample cut of the clothes, which she made herself, designed to distract from the weight she had put on over the years—not fat so much as a thickening around her torso and hips and a growing dewlap on her upper arms. There was even a small one forming under her chin. With the outfits it was almost impossible to tell how much of what you saw was middle-aged spread or simply the layered, oversized clothes.

And all the outfits were Parisian-chic, widow-weeds black.

"Who would you have preferred I name him after?"

The sound of a dam bursting: "Anybody but that no-count son of that W.I. woman across the street whose name I refuse to let cross my lips. Old monkey chaser from the islands! Cover your ears, baby"—she turned briefly to Sonny. "I promised myself I wasn't gonna do or say anything to spoil our first visit, but I can't help it. Been holding in too much too long!

"That so-and-so ran off with my only child and ruined her chances. A star! My baby could've been a star! Another Lena Horne—she was from Brooklyn too. Or Dorothy Dandridge.

You know that, you! Hattie! Cherisse had the looks, the voice, the personality. Could sing, act, and dance up a storm from the time she was little. You couldn't tell me she wasn't headed for Broadway and Hollywood, both!"

His *vedette* grandmother. That's who the woman was talking about. His *vedette*, movie star grandmother he called her, although he had never known her. At home, Hattie kept as many pictures of her, of her pretty face, as she did of the great Sonny-Rett Payne, the grandfather he'd been named after. She accorded equal space to them both.

". . . That fool robbed her of all that. Then after he ran off with her and had her all to himself over there in Paris, France, he turned her against me. Her own mother! Had her so she wouldn't write or call or send so much as a post-card. Years and years with never a word! She didn't even let me know when this child's mother was born. A grandbaby I never got to see or hear about . . ."

His girl-mother. She was talking now about the girl-mother he had also never known. Who hadn't even taken the trouble to name him before disappearing when he was only a week old. She had left the naming to Hattie. Suddenly he wished he could do as the woman had ordered and stopper his ears. He wished Hattie wasn't so far across the room.

". . . How could you let her do me like that, you! Hattie! You could've gotten her to write or call. Cherisse always listened to you more than to me." Said with a deep, galling resentment she could no longer contain. "My own child turning her back on me 'cause I told her she wasn't doing nothing but throwing her life away running behind some man who would never make a living playing a piano the way he did. And wasn't I right? Look how he ended up! Look how he died!"

Hattie's face was a window with the shade drawn all the way down. Nothing to be seen there. She was ready to leave though. Sonny saw the signs. She had placed her large tote bag of a pocketbook upright on her lap and adjusted her turban. You never saw her without one of her dramatically tied "Sikh turbans" as she called them. And like everything she wore, each one of them was black.

He too wanted to leave. The woman talking that way about his grandfather, his namesake and hero! He edged away from her on the sofa.

"And now here comes his brother gonna put on a big concert in his name." She hadn't ceased. "Somebody long dead and forgotten! Nobody listens to that crazy music of his anymore. Why's he bothering? What's behind it? That's what I'd like to know. But big shot Edgar Payne can afford to put on a concert or anything else what with the money he makes buying and selling these houses around here.

"Him and his Three R's Group!" Uttered with scorn beyond measure. "Gang is more like it. A gang of thieves and he's the ringleader. Going around pressuring people to sell him their old rundown houses cheap and also buying the ones the City's done condemned for just a dollar sometimes, the City's so glad to get rid of them, then fixing them up quick with money the banks are foolish enough to lend him and reselling them for a fortune. Always wheeling and dealing. I don't know anybody more underhanded. Nothing's beyond that W.I. He's worse than Tricky Dick Nixon had to resign . . ."

Sonny longed for his drawing *bloc*. Whenever he was around Big People talking talking talking and he couldn't fathom what they were talking about or he understood but wasn't interested or they were saying things that upset him—

as the woman was doing—or there was no *télé* around he could watch, he would take out his drawing *bloc* and pencil case and get to work on a castle or a fortress. Once he got started, he no longer heard the talk around him.

But today as they were setting out, Hattie had said no. He was meeting these people for the first time (she had called the unknown relatives "these people"), and it wouldn't look right for him to be sitting up there drawing.

"Know one thing: he needs to take some of that money he's got and put that mother of his away somewhere. Woman's got some of everything wrong with her, beginning with not being right in the head. And hear-tell she keeps a *nasty* house!"

The other great-grandmother woman, who he had decided might not be so bad after all. He shifted farther away on the sofa.

Across the room Hattie looked at her watch and rose to her feet, unmistakably ready to leave now.

She went unnoticed.

"An old crow! She's the reason that son of hers ran off with my baby. She's the one to blame. Just put her *away!*

"Her and all those other old W.I.s! Came flooding in here years ago and ruined the block. That's why I don't go out any-more, you know. Can't bear to see what they've done to Macon Street and all the streets around here. And now here comes Mr. Big Shot trying to undo the damage. For a profit naturally. Every time you look he's throwing up another scaffold, fixing up some old place to make a mint off of it . . ."

The woman going on and on, her voice a hurricane-force wind battering her slight, bowed frame; her rage des-ecrating her *palais royal* room.

✦ ✦ ✦

"Bet you're thinking I don't like this great-grandma. She talks too much."

It was noon, the visit over, and the woman stood, a penitent before him in her marble vestibule, the varicolored leaded glass in the fanlight above them glowing a stained-glass blue, yellow, and a medieval red in the sun that had finally emerged.

Hattie had already fled and stood waiting for him on the sidewalk. Before leaving, she had been instructed to bring him back three days hence, on Thursday, for the tour guide talk.

"All that running off at the mouth," the woman said, her head with the bobbed, dyed russet hair bowed, the cover girl lipstick bleeding into the fjord-like wrinkles around her mouth. "Couldn't help it, though. It's been too much too long. But I went and spoiled our visit, didn't I? So ashamed of myself. Think you can forgive me? Didn't mean to say anything hurtful. Say you forgive me. Please. Pretty please . . ."

He kept his eyes lowered and his mouth shut. Talking about his grandfather like that!

His unforgiving silence held until, desperate, she suddenly cried, "I know what! Instead of you calling me Great-Grandma, which is so old-sounding, I'm gonna let you call me by my name, Florence Varina. That way it'll be kinda like we're friends the same age. It's what my daddy always called me. I was Flo to everyone else, but Florence Varina to him. Now, besides my daddy, you'll be the only other person in the whole wide world to call me by my rightful name. How about that? Sound good to you?"

He nodded, but only so's she'd let him go.

Grateful, she gave him a parting hug with the arms not much longer than his. Her wonderful smell. "I'm gonna make it up to you, baby," she said. "I promise. I'm gonna see to it that the two of us have some good times together before you go back to Paris, France."

Finally, a whisper in his ear: "You don't know it, but I been holding on waiting for you."

He didn't understand.

"What's a W.I.?"

Hattie sighed and drew him close to her side. "A West Indian," she said. "Y'know, like the father of your friend Jean-Jacques who's from Martinique. She was just being mean to your other relatives saying it that way. That woman. She hasn't changed."

They were standing out in front of the house, waiting for Edgar Payne. Earlier he had arranged to pick them up after the second visit and take them to lunch. Florence Varina was seeing them off from the doorway at the top of the stoop, a fur coat draped around her shoulders and the maid, Dora, hovering protectively behind.

"Do you know that this is the first time I've ever been inside that house?" A suppressed outburst—Hattie sounding as if it had been too much too long for her also. "Here your grandmother and I were best friends from junior high school, yet Florence Varina McCullum-Jones would never so much as let me enter the front yard of Two fifty-eight."

Why? He was about to ask why when he spotted the car that had brought them from the airport two days ago.

The moment it pulled over, the double-leaf door at the head of the stoop slammed shut.

4

*"Sometimes shaking hands with the right folks
can make a big difference in this life.
Remember that, okay? It might come in handy
one of these days."*

So far, there were a couple of things Sonny liked about the
man who was the first of the relatives he had met. First,
there was his big, smooth-riding American car that had
ample room on the front seat to accommodate both him
and Hattie, with him sitting in the middle. Second, there was
the large, domed ring on the man's right hand. He'd never
seen a ring that size. Or one that had writing and tiny Roman
numerals inscribed on it, as well as what looked like a coat of
arms on top. It was the kind of ring the laird of a castle
might have used to affix his seal to the edicts that went forth
from his hand.

He liked it. In the car on the way to lunch, he examined
it in detail again out of the corner of his eye.

As for the man himself—his height: he appeared to be
as tall sitting down as when he was standing; his voice:
Sonny could feel it reverberating in his chest like the bass
drum in a parade seated beside him now on the front seat;

his face: a vague reminder of his grandfather's in the pictures at home; his head: bald, monumentally bald, with a wreath of pepper-and-salt hair laid at its base—this man, his great-uncle, the owner of the car and the ring and the house where he and Hattie were staying, which was on the same block of Macon Street as the two he had just visited, was too outsize, too overwhelming for him to assess as yet. He didn't even know what to call him, either out loud or in the privacy of his thoughts.

The man seemed to have anticipated his problem. When introducing himself at the airport, he had suggested that he call him Uncle Edgar. Great-Uncle Edgar was too much of a mouthful. Or even Uncle Ed would do, he'd said.

"But only when it feels right to you," he had added.

Sonny wasn't sure it would ever feel right, and so he had taken to calling him simply "the man" to himself, or sometimes, formally, the Edgar Payne man.

The restaurant Edgar Payne chose for them to have lunch was on a long commercial avenue that bordered Macon Street to the west. Reid Avenue it was called. It was a seedy, down-at-the-heels strip where many of the small businesses and storefronts, as well as the four- and five-story walk-ups tiered above them, stood boarded up or burnt out. A thin crowd of shoppers appeared as dispirited as their surroundings. As did the loungers outside the liquor stores and the bars that were already open, and the small knots of men and women either already nodding or waiting to score on some of the corners they drove past.

"Reid Avenue, Reid Avenue, it's a hundred times worse than I remember it," Hattie exclaimed in dismay, her gaze out the passenger window.

Edgar Payne, guiding the Lincoln Continental through the noon traffic, nodded. "It is. The sixties really did it in. All the burn-baby-burn rioting. Our folks justifiably angry, but harming themselves more than anyone else, seemed like. Reid Avenue still hasn't recovered. It's got a long way to go but my group is working on it."

As proof, he presented them with the restaurant minutes later. A renovated double storefront with a striped awning outside, a bright, freshly painted interior with comfortable booths and Boston ferns hanging in the windows, it was a modest oasis amid the blight.

"For years there wasn't a decent place to have lunch around here." This as he led them inside. "But as I said we're working on Reid Avenue."

The restaurant was owned by his Three R's Group.

"So how did the visits go?" Edgar Payne asked.

"Okay."

Hungry, Sonny was busy tackling something called a hero sandwich the man had ordered for him, as a reward, he joked, for the heroic morning he must have put in visiting the two old women. The thing was almost as long as his forearm, shaped like a submarine and crammed with enough sandwich meat and sliced cheese to last him for a week had he been home. Hattie who knew how to stretch their food would have seen to that.

"And my mother . . . ? Were you okay with her? I hope she didn't do anything to upset you . . ."

"No."

"Well, he certainly made out better than me. She made it clear I wasn't welcome. Wouldn't open the basement gate till I left."

Hattie still offended by how she'd been treated.

"I apologize for my mother," Edgar Payne said. "But I'm sure you remember how difficult she can be."

"Don't I! We couldn't even jump rope outside your house. She'd come storming out and chase us away like she owned the sidewalk!"

"Well, things are far worse now that her mind isn't what it used to be. There's no reasoning with her anymore . . ." He paused, reluctant perhaps to confide in Hattie, given the fact she had been away so long; but then clearly troubled, despairing, he was saying, "My mother shouldn't be living alone, not in her condition. But all I beg, she refuses to come stay with me and the family. And she won't hear of an adult or nursing home. She ran me out when I brought it up once. Nor can I get her to go to the doctor about the Parkinson's. Nor will she let me hire someone to look after her and the house. I make sure to keep up the exterior, so the place won't be another eyesore on the block, but inside is a disgrace and she won't let me touch it. All I'm good for is to see to it her old player piano still works.

"Ulene Payne! I can't tell you how impossible she's become!"

Someone had to defend her, so putting down the mammoth sandwich, Sonny announced once again, "She showed me how to play it, her piano, and it was fun."

"You two really got along, didn't you!" Edgar Payne turned to him, amazed. A relieved smile replaced his despair. "Let's see, I bet I know how she did it."

Before he could prepare himself, the man's arms went around him from behind, the hands—one with the great seal of a ring—took up his hands and, after arranging them as his mother had done, sent them racing under his along the edge of the table.

He laughed. The outsize hands riding piggyback on his. Colossal arms encircling him. Larger-than-life face bent close to his. The man smell. A different, more powerful aura that wasn't about creams and lotions.

Hattie looked on. When they came in, Edgar Payne had quickly seated her first, then placed Sonny and himself opposite her in the booth. Now, across from them, she sat looking on and smiling, the age lines around her mouth turned to laugh lines again. Hattie smiling, yet at the same time, unawares, frowning slightly. A faint crease of a frown had alighted like a subliminal query on the smooth mocha-colored skin of her forehead. Her skin. It had been the best feature of her otherwise ordinary, "around the block" face when she was young. And it still was now that she was in her late fifties. *"Ta peau! Merveilleuse! Pas une ride!* Your skin! Marvelous! Not a wrinkle!" "Melanin," she'd say, although the French usually didn't know what that was. *"Beaucoup, beaucoup de* melanin."

"That's the way your grandfather learned how to play," the man was saying, the demonstration over. He had withdrawn his hands, his arms. "Did you know that?"

"No."

"Well, that's how. When he was small he used to sit for hours chasing after those keys, pretending he was the one playing, with my mother an adoring audience of one. I could never understand what he got out of it. I know one thing: by the time he started taking lessons he already knew how to play.

"Did you see his picture on top the piano?"

"Yes." The boy in the old-timey suit. His grandfather,

part of whose stage name he bore. He had figured as much. He had enlisted his help with the playing.

He turned his attention back to the sandwich.

"You don't have to eat all of that big thing," Hattie said. The faint query of a frown remained.

"And what about your other great-grandmother?"

Lunch over, they were on their way to visit Edgar Payne's office, the early afternoon sun traveling overhead at the same speed as the car, while the wind that had lost much of its force over the course of the morning struggled to keep up.

"You haven't said anything about her. I bet she talked your ears off."

"She told me to cover them so's not to hear her."

The man laughed and waited for him to go on.

He left it at that though. He didn't know why, he couldn't have given a reason, but he suddenly decided he wasn't telling on her either, the Florence Varina woman, never mind all the mean things she'd said. Let Hattie tell if she wanted to, but not him.

Which she promptly did. "You would've wanted to cover your ears too if you'd heard what she had to say about you and that group of yours. Certain practices you all go in for. She had quite a list."

"I can well imagine."

"Like pressuring people to sell."

"Sometimes," he said. "Especially when they won't keep up their property. Nothing's pure."

"And the big money you make off each deal."

"Sometimes. Nothing's wholly selfless." He shrugged, paused. Then: "Look, we're doing *some* good! You don't know it, but people who gave up on the place when things really went downhill are slowly coming back, some of them. You see it more and more. You even see a number of young people moving in, young folks who understand it's up to us to save what's ours. I tell you, it does my heart good. And I'm not being sentimental."

"You'd never know any of this listening to Mis' McCullum-Jones."

"Look," he repeated, "don't expect a kind word about me or anything I'm associated with from that woman. As she sees it, I'm the Shylock of Central Brooklyn. Her problem is that she's still waging the American–West Indian War. As if a people in our situation can afford that kind of divisive nonsense."

Said with disgust and a hopeless shake of his head.

Minutes later, he drew up before a two-story commercial building on the same long avenue. Like the storefront restaurant, the building had been renovated and updated with a new façade of permastone and tinted glass. The entrance door, though, was a Victorian grace note, a beautifully restored, highly polished double-leaf door with carved trompe l'oeil paneling and a Tiffany glass fanlight. It easily rivaled the one at 258 Macon.

The Three R's Group of Central Brooklyn
Reclamation. Restoration. Rebirth.

Sonny could read only the top line on the sign above the door.

"Not bad," Hattie said, looking around the office. "Naturally yours is much bigger than the others we saw."

There was this edge to her voice.

Edgar Payne ignored it. "Naturally," he said.

He had just taken them on a brief tour of the building and along the way he had stopped to introduce them to the other principal members of the group. They were middle-aged men like himself in dark business suits, and one or two women. All of them were from around the block, in the wider meaning of their part of Brooklyn. One of the men remembered Hattie. They had gone to the same high school.

Afterward, Edgar Payne brought them to his office. And it was true what she said: his was much larger than the others. The spacious room was literally three rooms, an actual office, then a sitting room complete with sofa and chairs, drapes at the windows and paintings on the walls, and beyond this, a conference area.

In the office section, Hattie immediately went over to inspect two photographs on the desk.

"Ha," she said. "Everybody always knew you'd marry Alva!"

Sonny at her side gave a look. He saw a smiling woman with glasses, a close cap of curly graying hair, and a face that looked almost as white as Madame Molineaux's. She was standing in a garden in full bloom before a two-story columned house that stretched beyond the picture's frame.

Hattie: "Little quiet Alva lived over Perlman's drugstore on Reid Avenue. You could hardly ever get a word out of her as I remember."

Edgar Payne: "Don't worry, she found her voice over the years."

"And looks like you've got yourself quite a spread."

"It's Alva's spread," he said. "I would've been perfectly content to remain on Macon Street, but she always wanted out of Brooklyn and believe me, she wasn't quiet about it. So when I got a good deal on a place through one of my contacts, she got her house on Long Island, complete with that garden you see, which is her passion, and I kept our old place on the block, renting it out except for my little pied-à-terre on the top floor where I stay when I work late and don't feel like facing that long drive out to the island. We respect each other's turf, Alva and I, which is probably why we get along so well."

The other picture on the desk was of their daughter and her children, a small boy and an older girl. His daughter, Edgar Payne said, was divorced and going to law school in Atlanta. Her children lived with him and his wife.

"Alva and I are back to being parents in our old age. But we don't mind. In fact, we're doing a much better job this time around. We didn't do so good with our daughter. But then she was a handful."

This to Hattie. And to Sonny: "Bet you didn't know you had some second cousins your age, did you?"

He shook his head. He had never been told about them. About any of the relatives in America. *Pourquoi?* Why? Hattie must have her reasons.

"You'll be spending this weekend with them, so you can get in some playtime. That all right with you?"

"Yes," he said. He was already beginning to miss Jean-Jacques.

"Of course we had hoped you'd be staying longer. That way you could've spent more time with your cousins. With all of us, in fact. But that's not to be."

What he meant was that Hattie was limiting the visit to two weeks. Two weeks before the concert and perhaps—but only perhaps—a few days after it was over. They had arrived on Saturday. Today was Monday. The concert would be a week from this Friday. Two of the fourteen days were already gone.

"We're gonna keep it short and sweet," she had said once she decided not to tear up the letter and the check and consign them to the Seine.

"Anyway, we're happy to have you with us if only for a day," the man said and then both startled and pleased him by bestowing a playful little uppercut on his chin.

It was as light as a caress.

There were many other pictures in the office, and Hattie, Sonny in tow, headed for the wall behind the desk. There, on display amid a collection of plaques, framed citations, and awards, was a veritable gallery of photographs showing Edgar Payne with any number of important-looking people, nearly all of them white. Edgar Payne smiling with them, shaking hands with them, and in many instances accepting checks from them, some of the checks blown up giant-size.

She came to a halt in front of the largest of the pictures which hung directly behind his desk.

"Oh-la-la! Bobby Kennedy, no less!"

The image that caused her outcry showed a younger, 1960s Edgar Payne who still had most of his hair, smiling and shaking hands with Robert Kennedy. Kennedy with the toothy grin and cowlick of a twelve-year-old and the steely, purposefully directed gaze of his calling.

"Don't tell me you actually knew him?"

"Not only knew him, but worked for him."

"Oh?"

"A long story."

Before going on, he led them around to the front of the

desk and seated them there, then settled himself in the desk chair opposite. A globed light overhead shone down on the bald dome of his head and on his face below, a face whose features—broad, flared nose, heavy lips, high forehead—might have been carved out of the same dark sandstone as the houses he bought and sold. And under the overhang of his brow his slightly hooded eyes also hid something as purposefully directed, and even more unyielding, in his own gaze.

"Cat don't play!" is the way they would have put it around the block.

"All right, the long story."

There had been, he said, this Marshall-type plan, spearheaded by Kennedy when he was the senator from New York, to entirely rebuild Central Brooklyn—"Or what our detractors like to call Bed-Stuy, a name I never use. I call it Central Brooklyn, the heart of the borough. That's the way I've thought of it from a kid"—and as someone already in urban planning, already trying to salvage the old neighborhood—"Florence McCullum isn't the only one who loves this place!"—he had suddenly found himself in on the ground floor of the most sweeping renewal project ever undertaken anywhere.

"Ulene Payne's boychild in the right place at the right time." His laugh. He became, he said, part of the senator's inner circle on the project. He was among those who helped research and draft the proposal. And when it was finally approved by Washington, he was the one chosen to head up the huge housing program . . .

"You mean you didn't hear about it over there in Paris?" Now his voice had the edge to it. *Touché.*

"No," said Hattie.

He went on. "As for the millions-plus needed over the years for the miracle to happen? No worry. The senator vowed to keep the pipeline from Washington open. Because apart from any rich-boy altruism on his part, there were the politics of the thing: the Central Brooklyn Renewal Plan was to be a major showpiece in his bid for the White House.

"Nothing's pure. Nothing's wholly selfless." His credo again.

"And do you know we actually got it halfway off the ground . . ."

"And then they killed him too." Hattie.

"Yep. The bloodletting just wouldn't quit. And with him gone and then old LBJ gone and Nixon in charge, we soon found ourselves on our own. The pipeline all but dried up. We'd have to look elsewhere for money, we knew, if we wanted to continue even on a small scale. That's when I put that picture you see behind me up on the wall, right above my head. As collateral."

"Collateral?"

"Yep. Just that. It's helped us get many a loan. The people from the banks come in here, see me and Kennedy shaking hands—they can't miss it sitting where you are—and they're more disposed to approve the loan and hand over the check. Our reputation and track record help, of course—we've been at it a long time—but nothing quite does it like that shot of me and the senator."

Suddenly, startling him, the man's hand closed around his. He'd been sitting there thinking Big People talking again and fighting sleep, the sandwich heavy in his stomach, when the Edgar Payne man suddenly reached across his desk, swallowed up his hand in his own, and began shaking it. And he wasn't being playful as with the uppercut before. He was shaking his hand seriously, treating him almost as if he were one of the important-looking people on the wall.

And with equal seriousness, he was saying, looking him in the eye, "Sometimes shaking hands with the right folks can make a big difference in this life. Remember that, okay? It might come in handy one of these days."

"Okay," he said to accommodate him. He didn't really understand.

Edgar Payne continued to hold his hand. He had become suddenly thoughtful, abstracted.

"Not that I like it all that much—the hand shaking and smiling. Truthfully, I wish it were otherwise. That we had our own banks and loan companies, our own resources, so I wouldn't always have to be running after these people skinning my teeth, saying 'Please, massa' with my hand 'long out' as my mother would put it . . .

"By the way, did you have any trouble understanding her?"

"Sometimes."

"It's her accent. Anyway, let's hope you and my grandchildren won't have to do all the smiling and begging. That's what I'm trying my best to make happen. Right now, though, my little group doesn't have a choice. It's the only way we can find the wherewithal to get the job done, which is to take the beat-up old houses you see around here that were once beautiful and make them as close to beautiful again as possible, so people like us will have someplace nice to live. Think that's a good idea?"

He thought of Hattie's many complaints about where they lived and said yes.

Perhaps to impress all this on him, Edgar Payne kept on

holding his hand across the varnished surface of the desk. He only relinquished it when Hattie, who had been silently looking on, her eye on the joined hands, abruptly stood up and said, "Jet lag. I could use a nap. So could Sonny."

5

*"I've been a walker in the city
from way back."*

The man's pied-à-terre apartment where they were staying, on the top floor of his house on Macon Street, was perfect in every way but one: it lacked a *télé*. This Sonny found a major disappointment. And he couldn't even bring up the subject to the man, perhaps ask him to rent one for their stay, because before leaving home Hattie had made it clear that there were certain things he was not to talk about, among them their own lack of a *télé*, a telephone, a decent refrigerator, stereo, and kitchen stove. They would have all those things and more she said once she could put her hands on some real money.

Nor was he to mention the Club Violette where she worked, her job as *habilleuse* or wardrobe mistress to get the girls—who were billed as *danseuses exotiques*—quickly in and out of their costumes between the constant shows and to keep the skimpy garments in good repair. Nor was there any need for him to bring up the fact—and she had stressed this—that the Violette had been closed down again by the authorities shortly before they left for the States.

The same prohibition held true for where they lived. No mention was to be made of what she called their little ghetto *deux pièces sans confort:* their two-room apartment on the top floor at 130, rue Sauffroy, where the toilet which they shared with his *nounou* next door was out on the landing.

Even his *nounou,* Madame Molineaux, was on the list of no-nos, specifically what Hattie called her "love affair with Monsieur Père Magloire," Père Magloire being the brand name of the Calvados the old woman drank, she said, to ease her many ailments.

He was to keep quiet about that too.

"Those people over there don't have to know all of our business, okay?"

"Okay." What else to say? Hattie had her reasons for things. Sometimes he asked *pourquoi?* why? and got an answer. This time he sensed it would be futile.

He awoke from the nap to find her in the living room at the front of the apartment. Hattie didn't appear to have slept. She was sitting waiting for him in the man's special chair, a laird's kingly lounge chair, which the man called a BarcaLounger. It was where he said he did his serious thinking and listening. By listening he meant the sizable collection of record albums and CD re-releases neatly shelved on either side of the large stereo system in the room.

All the recordings bore his grandfather's name.

"Good Lord, you must have every record he ever made!"

The sight of the collection had brought Hattie to a standstill as she entered the apartment the day they arrived.

"I do. I think I managed to track down every last one of them. And I've got a duplicate of each one you see here in the house out on the island."

She had given Edgar Payne an odd look, had started to say or ask him something, then changed her mind.

She sat now in the man's special chair, their coats on her lap.

Time for their daily walk. Not even being away from Paris was to change that.

At home, before leaving for work in the evenings, Hattie regularly went for a walk, taking Sonny with her. She did not allow him to go out to play after school—too many bad elements on rue Sauffroy—and so to make up for it, she took him walking with her. The daily stroll took place even in the rain. Not in a downpour certainly, but the chilly, gray, off-and-on light rains that plagued the city like a watery mistral winter and spring seldom deterred her. Rain, rain, rain, Hattie would fuss. A city nearly always in tears. Whoever called it gay? Complaining, but with affection. The weeping skies that hung for weeks above the famous roofs, the funereal look and feel to the air in season, that too, she said, was dear old Paree.

Their street, poor, abject, treeless rue Sauffroy with its crumbling walk-ups that looked as if they predated even the *Ancien Régime;* rue Sauffroy, with its erupted, crippling paving stones, choked gutters, and ragtag laundry hung out front to dry, was not considered part of the evening walk. Nor was the noisy commercial avenue nearby which catered to the mostly Arab and African denizens of the *quartier,* those who were legal and possessed a precious *Carte de résident* as well as the numerous illegals or *sans papiers:* no papers.

Making their escape, they first had to negotiate the avenue with its cheap-goods, garish stores, swarming open-air market, and smoke-filled cafés—the cafés the refuge of the old men of the desert in their Yasir Arafat kaffiyehs, whiling away the day over glasses of hot, sugar-laced tea. Hurrying past the *boucherie* where Hattie bought their small weekly supply of meat, they were greeted by the gargoyle grin of the sheep's head in the rotisserie out front. An entire sheep's head—huge, soulful eyes and teeth intact—was always to be seen roasting alongside the trussed-up chickens on the spit.

When Sonny was small and had gotten over being scared of the slowly browning eyes and the skeleton grin, he used to practice his numbers in both English and French by counting the two long rows of roasting teeth while, inside the shop, Hattie and Monsieur Benhabib, the butcher, haggled over the price of the cheapest cuts of meat.

In their flight each evening, they also had to dodge the *sans papiers* touts or runners busy on the sidewalk handing out the flyers and business cards of their employers, the local marabous: Monsieur Sobgui Teno of Cameroon, Monsieur Moussa Sene Mambety of Senegal, Monsieur Cheick Omar Diakite of Mali, and all the other marabous from Africa below the Sahara who, according to the flyers and business cards, possessed the power to change bad luck to good, sickness to health, and loneliness to love for a fee.

The touts, the runners, transplanted goatherds and village boys, silhouette-black and rail-thin in their long traditional djellabahs and kufi skullcaps, knew it was useless to ply Hattie with the notices. *Une Américaine noire.* A nonbeliever.

The avenue, with four wide, dangerous lanes of two-way traffic, marked the boundary of their *quartier* to the east. Once Hattie crossed them at the light and they reached the other side, they were officially in another *quartier,* one in which the white domes of the Basilica of Sacré-Coeur could be glimpsed high on its hill in the distance.

Here, the evening walk also officially began. Because here, after walking several blocks farther east, another world presented itself. Broad, tree-lined avenues that were called boulevards and not just simply avenues as in their part of town, well-kept squares where real Parisians speaking proper French could be seen in the cafés. Clean-swept, uncrowded residential streets and flanking the streets, rows of grand late-nineteenth-century apartment buildings, the renowned Parisian *immeubles,* that in their height and girth and the prow-like thrust of their exteriors called to mind the great transatlantic ocean liners of the same bygone century, the dowager ships of the rich.

The thing Sonny liked most about the *immeubles* were the bas-relief stone heads, the *mascarons,* to be found above nearly every one of the huge entrance doors they passed. Each carved head, animal or human, was different, and Hattie had explained them all to him in detail. One was a scowling Bluebeard, another a benign Père Noël face, next a peasant girl. There was a snarling lion missing one of its incisors, a wild-haired Beethoven lookalike, and a Janus head, the two bearded faces back to back: Janus, god of doorways, she had told him. Her favorite was a *mascaron* of Joan of Arc, her two long pigtails pulled forward and crossed like a brace of swords under her chin: Joan ready to do battle for God, king, and country, she said. His was a mustachioed Hessian soldier whom the sculptor had made a freak, in that he had given him grapes instead of ears. On either side of the stone head where the ears should have been there hung a large bunch of grapes.

"How come?" He had stood openmouthed the first time he looked up and saw it. He must have been three or four at the time.

"The artist just felt like it."

Hattie. She always had an answer.

She had once lived, she often told him, along with his grandfather and grandmother, the three of them always together, in an *immeuble* twice as grand as the ones on their walk. It had been a majestic old building she said, with its classic mansard roof slanted toward the sky, an elevator in the design of a birdcage, and a ship's proud thrust to its exterior that gave the impression it was about to weigh anchor and set sail at any moment.

Best of all, her *immeuble* had been across the river in Paree Cinq, near the Luxembourg, the Sorbonne, the movie theaters at Odéon, and the clubs, the jazz clubs where Sonny-Rett Payne had once played, where he had reigned. To this day, there hung a large picture of him, like a billboard, outside the Club Belle Epoque on rue Monge, kept there in homage to him.

Sonny had seen it: his grandfather enshrined larger-than-life above the entrance to the nightclub. Every year on his birthday Hattie took him to visit it. Last year when he was eight she had borrowed a camera from Madame N'Dour, their Senegalese neighbor on the fourth floor in their building, and taken a picture of him standing like a sentry below the image.

Soon's she put her hands on some real money—Hattie's constant refrain—they'd be moving back across the river, back to the heart of the city. It was the only place to live.

Sonny wasn't altogether sure he wanted to go; to leave everything he was used to: his *nounou*, for one, whom he loved; for another, his tiny room in the *deux pièces sans confort,* where Hattie had hung a blown-up copy of the picture of him outside the Club Belle Epoque; his school (which Hattie also used the word "ghetto" to describe) where he was good at reading, drawing, and *"le foot"*—or what was properly called soccer. There was also his best friend at school, Jean-Jacques Rosette. And what about the *mascaron* soldier and his two bunches of grapes? He'd miss him too.

True, living on the other side of the river he'd be closer to his once-famous grandfather. But then hadn't he finally found a secret way to keep him nearby and safe, so that the bad dreams he had about him didn't come so often anymore?

At dusk, the walk finished, they bought a baguette and returned home. He was always given the long loaf to carry and he held it upright, the way he would a lance. Every so often Hattie reached over and pinched a morsel off the heel of the bread, one morsel for him, one for herself, another for him, popping them into his mouth like a mother bird. Sometimes by the time they arrived back on rue Sauffroy the baguette would be a quarter less than its original size.

"Pourquoi? Je te demande pourquoi. Chaque soir une promenade! Each evening a walk! Why? And always dragging the poor child along! *Même quand il fait froid!* Even in the cold! Even in the rain! *Quelle bêtise!* What idiocy!

"Give me my handsome little man, my treasure!"

Madame Molineaux snatching him to her, claiming him as her own.

She periodically scolded Hattie about the walks, her aged head with its side-to-side tic that gave the impression she was always saying *non, non, non* to everything underscoring her disapproval, her breath ripe with the smell of Père Magloire's fermented apples. She herself never went out, except once a month to collect her pension check from the post office. Otherwise, no. Her age. Her arthritic knees. The six flights of treacherous stairs. The broken lights on the stairs . . .

Mais surtout les sales Algériens! But most of all the dirty Algerians! They had killed the cream of France in their stupid war and now that they were free, independent, instead of staying in the desert where they belonged, they were pouring into la belle France (a large tricolor hung above her front door), into Paris, into *le quartier.* They had ruined it, *le quartier.* She had lived and worked here all her life and they had ruined it. The dirt. The street thieves. The drugs. The sheeps' heads roasting on the sidewalk. *Les barbares!* They were nothing but barbarians. No, she did not, would not, go out among them in the streets. Nor should Hattie, especially taking the child with her.

"Je te demande pourquoi."

"I've been a walker in the city from way back" was all Hattie ever offered by way of an answer, speaking in her make-do French that sometimes caused Madame Molineaux to clap her hands over her ears in horror.

With the afternoon light ebbing, Hattie handed Sonny his coat, enveloped herself in hers, and the long day not yet over, she led him down the two flights of stairs inside the house, then down the tall stoop outside to the yard below and through the front gate back onto Macon Street.

They had the long block virtually to themselves, the rush hour not under way yet, and only a few children out playing after school—they were the first Sonny had seen for the day. As if to accommodate them further, the morning chill was gone and the wind scarcely resembled its earlier self.

Hattie confined the walk to the one block, her steps tracing a course that took them repeatedly up one side of the street, then down the other. For the visits that morning, she had hurried him along, scarcely looking around her. Now, moving slowly, she was carefully inspecting the old houses, her gaze under the Sikh turban searching their lineaments as if trying to tease out what had happened within their walls during the thirty-plus years she'd been gone.

Silent. She walked in silence, looking. An occasional gust tugged at her coat, a black, voluminous cape-like affair with her standard wide-wide dolman sleeves. When he was small Sonny used to worry that one day those sleeves would suddenly turn into giant wings and take her soaring out of sight, leaving him utterly alone behind.

Hattie: fathermothersisterbrother.

Near the western end of the block, looking toward Manhattan and Jersey, she finally stopped in front of one of the brownstones being renovated, its façade partly hidden by the scaffolding already in place.

"Two thirty-three," she said, speaking for the first time. "That's where I lived. Up on the third floor with that old Mis' Dawson . . ."

Hattie's voice adrift. Her eyes also. She wasn't really talking to him. It often happened. He knew, by now, to simply wait until she returned from wherever she had drifted off to and noticed him again. So he looked up the block to where the children were playing. They had started a helter-skelter game of *chat*, which he knew from Hattie was called tag in English, and in his head he went running, darting, and dodging with them.

*   *   *

"I was with her the longest . . ."

So long, in fact, the other kids on Macon Street forgot she was a City child. That Mis' Dawson, who once had a husband but never any children, had been prevailed upon by her church, St. Peter Claver, Catholic, Colored, to open her roomy third-floor apartment as well as her heart to one of the City's children. The woman reluctantly took her; then, because Hattie could pretty much look after herself, Mis' Dawson kept her so long she became just another kid around the block. And she was considered a lucky one at that because she got to stay out late when the woman went to bingo in the evenings.

She had her a bingo jones, Mis' Dawson, but she wasn't all that bad when compared to some of the other "mothers" she'd lived with. That short-tempered Mis' Rayburn for one. The woman so quick with her hand or the strap. You didn't have to do anything and she'd be upside your head. Or that old West Indian Mis' Motley on Jefferson Avenue who had two other City children besides herself. Dinner was invariably the surplus cabbage and navy beans the government gave out free from a storefront on Fulton Street. And the money the City sent to feed and clothe them properly? Every penny went to pay the mortgage on her old house.

Mis' Hamilton on Decatur Street? Another cheapskate. She had tried turning her into a drayhorse at age seven, sending her with an old baby carriage up Reid Avenue to the icehouse. Woman too cheap to buy one of the new refrigerators with the motor on top. Her fear, her shame on the way back that some kid she knew would see her pushing the broken-down carriage with the 25-pound block of ice inside.

The only really nice one was Mis' Porter on Quincy Street.

She had treated her the same as her own two little girls. And she was the only one who ever took her out to Creedmoor State Hospital to visit her mother with the pretty name. Dawn. Dawn Carmichael. She used to wonder: Why hadn't her mother thought to give her that same pretty name? Instead, all she thought to do, they said, was to try and hurt herself and anyone around her, including her baby, so that the City had had to put her away.

On the train ride back from the hospital in Queens Mis' Porter would cradle her in her arms.

Nice. Mis' Porter was nice. But not her old husband who liked for her to touch him down there. Her hand forced around his thing whenever he caught her on the upstairs landing. It made her think of a cop's billy, it was that thick, long, and dark. And Mr. Porter breathing hard and making crybaby sounds as he worked her hand back and forth, back and forth as if it was a piston . . .

When she started wetting the bed at night, every night, Mis' Porter, nice as she was, had given her back to the City.

So she was glad for Mis' Dawson, never mind the bingo and the emptiness of the apartment when she hurried off in the early evening. Left alone, Hattie treated herself to a walk along Macon Street.

It would be the dinner hour then, all her friends inside having dinner in the basement dining room that faced the street. The lights would be on inside, but often the window shades were still up or the venetian blinds open, allowing her a look-see as she strolled by.

With some of the houses, there wasn't much to see. Like No. 301 where the two "E" brothers lived, that old Edgar thinks he's so smart always the first one with his hand up in class and his little goody-two-shoes kid brother Everett always practicing the piano and their mean old mother acting like she owns the City's sidewalks. Their dining room was a rented-out bedroom with the shades kept drawn. The woman and a lot of those other old West Indians changing over the houses into rooms and renting to any old body. Bringing down the block, the neighborhood, people said.

So there was nothing to see there. But across the street and a ways up the block, 258 was another story. The best house, the best dining room bar none. There, her steps slowed to a halt, her hungry gaze sidestepped the tree in the yard, stripped away the iron grating over the dining room windows, and, her dark face camouflaged by the gathering dusk, she feasted on the scene inside.

It was always the same: the three at a gleaming claw-and-ball-footed table under a brass chandelier shiny as gold, whose lights kept igniting little jeweled fires in the crystal, china, and silver-plate settings. The mother, Florence Varina McCullum-Jones, dressed each evening as if for a dinner party, and talking, hers the only lips seen moving most of the time; the father, Mr. Jones, a silent, uncomfortable-looking brownskin man who behaved like a stranger at his own table; and only child, Cherisse.

Stuck-up, show-off, siddity Cherisse who never came out to play. Too busy being taken to singing, dancing, and acting lessons after school. Too busy being taken shopping downtown. She the only one on the block wearing a Shirley Temple coat with a fur collar, muff, and hat. Too busy being escorted to the beauty parlor every other Saturday for the Shirley Temple curls, with a touch-up the week in between.

Sometimes peering at the tableau inside 258 from the hunter's blind provided her by the darkness, the longing Hattie felt would become so acute, so filled with anger she would want to rush inside, yank the show-off out of her chair, chase her from the dining room, from the house, from Macon Street even, just dispossess her utterly and install herself at the family table.

The stuck-up wanted nothing to do with any of them on the block, certainly not with someone like her, a City child, she was convinced. Until one evening in early spring. As she stood watching, spying, she saw to her disbelief Miss Siddity slowly turn away from Florence Varina talking nonstop and for a moment direct her gaze outside. Not that she could see out. The brightly lighted dining room and the dusk outdoors made the windows a one-way glass that favored Hattie. She could see clearly from the dark into the light.

Cherisse gazed out nonetheless, unable to see but looking anyway, even searching for her, the envious voyeur, Hattie imagined, and with a longing as profound as her own. If she had been brave enough, the milk-chocolate Shirley Temple might even have abandoned mother and father, the pretty room, and the best house on the block to join her on the sidewalk.

That was how she chose to read the look that lasted only seconds.

So that when, in junior high, they became friends she wasn't surprised. Hadn't she read it into being that spring night? And they were the kind of friends that prompted the other kids to say, "If you sees one, you know you *gots* to see the other!" They were that close. Being together at school wasn't enough, so that whenever they could—Cherisse going behind her mother's back and even lying when necessary—they stole more time after three o'clock upstairs at Mis' Dawson's before she came home from her nurse's aide job.

Sitting cross-legged facing each other on the bed in Hattie's room, they lovingly popped each other's doohickeys, painted each other's nails and toes and mouths flame red, sang along with the girl groups on the radio, got up from the bed and practiced their dancing—the lindy, the slow drag; laid back down and also practiced how to kiss and touch in ways that went beyond little kids playing doctor-and-nurse, Hattie losing her ordinary-looking self and becoming with each deep kiss and caress the much-loved, dressed-up, prized daughter at the dining room table. And because she was as smart as old Edgar P., his hand always the first one up, she helped her gift of a best friend with her homework, while Cherisse advised her on how to dress and how to fix her thick bush of hair.

(Mis' Dawson never once took the time to comb and braid it for her, never once sent her to the beauty parlor.)

Later, in high school, when Cherisse turned boy crazy and Hattie started working part-time in Birdell's record store on Reid Avenue (where to her surprise she discovered that goody-two-shoes Everett Payne was a regular customer on the sly), their friendship, hers and Cherisse's, and all of its attendant rituals, still came before all else.

Florence Varina was not pleased. "Is that the only friend you could find? Some foster care child? Couldn't you pick somebody better than that?"

Not only was Hattie barred from entering the yard at 258, but in years to come, when Sonny-Rett Payne became part of their friendship, Florence Varina would accuse her—Hattie—of aiding and abetting in what she—Florence Varina—considered to be a criminal act.

So too would Ulene Payne across the street at 301.

✦　　　✦　　　✦

"Could somebody please tell me what I'm doing back here? How I could've let myself be talked into coming near this place again?"

Hattie upset. He started to remind her of the reason for the trip. The concert. His grandfather. Although he wasn't sure that would suffice as an answer. So he did what he always did when she was upset or feeling low and didn't have her *médicaments* with her. To soothe her and to restore her to herself and to him, he quietly slipped his hand into hers.

It always worked.

"Hungry?" She was suddenly all maternal concern.

"Yes," he said, although most of the hero sandwich was still in his stomach.

At that, she began spanking herself on the back of the hand. "Bad, bad, bad-bad Hattie, letting her poor child starve!"

She used to do that when he was small—spank herself— to stop him when he cried. He was much too big for her to be doing it now; he nevertheless still liked it.

A sweeping apologetic hug in the wide-winged coat and then she was hurrying him back up Macon Street, the sun a mere reddish stain in the sky over Jersey and the falling dusk at their heels.

The children playing *chat* had disappeared indoors.

Hattie remained upset though. Because later that evening she took a few of her candy array of pink, yellow, blue, and cream-colored capsules, tablets, and pills. Her *médicaments* she called them. Some were to calm her, others to lift her spirits.

Her *médicaments* was another thing he was not to mention.

6

"I were there!"

Big People talking talking talking again.

This time the people were those in charge of putting on the concert. It was the following evening, Tuesday, and a number of them were gathered in the sitting area of the man's office, all of them talking at the same time. Or so it seemed to Sonny.

This time he was prepared. Hattie had allowed him to bring along his drawing *bloc,* and as always it was helping him to tune out the voices.

"What've you got there?" the man had asked when he came to collect them for the meeting. Hattie was still inside getting dressed, while he already had his coat on and was sitting waiting for the man in the BarcaLounger (he liked operating the lever which lowered and raised the padded and tufted backrest). The drawing *bloc* lay on his lap, the case with his special pencils stowed among its pages.

He told him what it was.

"Oh? Can I have a look?"

Usually he only showed his drawings to Hattie, Madame

Molineaux, and privately at school to Jean-Jacques. But this wasn't someone you refused, so he handed it over.

The hand with the huge ring slowly turned the pages. A smile slowly spread across the face high above him.

"Say, you're pretty good, but where'd you get the idea to draw all these castles?"

"From a book I got as a present."

The book, a big colorful picture storybook with page after page of medieval castles and fortresses and armored knights setting forth on their caparisoned horses to slay dragons and gorgons and to find something called the Holy Grail, had been among the secondhand toys, games, and books that the church in their *quartier,* St.-Joseph-des-Epinettes, collected from children elsewhere in the city and then, like a lending library, loaned to those like himself. Toys, games, and books that looked practically new, as well as used, expensive magazines for Big People like Hattie. He had borrowed the one book so often, they finally made him a present of it. Once it was his, he set about drawing the castles and fortresses inside. Using tracing paper, he painstakingly copied each one and afterward retraced it onto a page in the drawing *blocs* Hattie bought for him. After a while, when he found he could draw them reasonably well without having to first trace them, he began making up his own. Castles and fortresses of his own invention.

Hattie willingly kept him supplied with the drawing *blocs.* They were cheap enough. Besides, they made up she said for the *télé* they didn't have as yet.

"Soon's I put my hands on some real money . . ."

"And who's this in the corner on each page?" the man asked.

"Me."

He always drew a miniature version of himself in full armor, his visor down, in the bottom right-hand corner of every drawing. Himself armed with a lance, a wicked-looking halberd, or a Sir Lancelot broadsword.

"Kinda like your signature, eh?"

"Yes," he said and left it at that. He had never told anyone, not even Hattie or Madame Molineaux or Jean-Jacques, why he posted himself armed and in full armor on each page.

At the meeting the first thing the man did was to introduce him and Hattie around. Strange faces crowding in on him. Strange voices exclaiming over him. Too many hands reaching down to shake his hand, to pat his cheek, to tilt his chin up for a better look at him. And the talking talking talking already under way.

Out of the eddy of faces he registered only a few. A pretty lady, for one, with her hair in a short, bushy halo around her head. She liked his suit—it was another of the new ones Hattie had bought with the money the man had sent.

"Looks like you came dressed to take me out dancing tonight," she said, pretty eyes, pretty mouth smiling.

And he suddenly found himself wondering with the pretty face bent close to his: Did his runaway girl-mother maybe look anything like her? There were no pictures of her at home. According to what he sometimes overheard Hattie saying to Madame Molineaux those nights when she didn't work or the Violette had been closed down again—her anguished voice repeating what the old woman already knew—the runaway had destroyed every picture ever taken of her, even the ones when she was a baby, before she fled 130, rue Sauffroy at age fourteen, and then Paris itself a year later.

Nothing of her left behind but him.

Right away he felt the cruel balloon he secretly carried around in his chest begin to inflate, crowding his heart and lungs, his throat, and threatening to reach his eyes and explode in a babyish flood of tears.

That's what always happened when he thought of the runaway.

"Hattie Carmichael, Hattie Carmichael! All these years! Girl, how could you go and stay away so long? C'mere!"

A barrel-chested old man wearing dark dark sunglasses like somebody blind and with a hoarse boom of a voice was holding Hattie in a loving, albeit chiding, embrace.

"Shades Bowen! Still with the midnight glasses?"

"Girl, the world's still too much to take with the naked eye."

"I hear you. Oh, it's good to see you again!"

Hattie as lovingly returned his embrace.

Shades Bowen. He had earned his nickname, Hattie remembered, by being the first in junior high school to affect the opaque, ultra-cool, bebop sunglasses.

They held each other for a long time.

"Boy!" The man then turned the glasses on Sonny. "Do you know I used to blow tenor behind your grandfather? Me behind the great Sonny-Rett Payne! Did you know that?"

He shook his head no.

"And you know somethin' else? Come the concert next week Friday, I'm gonna be up on that stage trying my best old as I am to blow a little tenor behind his memory. C'mere!"

He found himself corralled in a massive embrace.

It was easy to remember Shades Bowen.

The same was true for the man he and Hattie met next, Edgar Payne's lawyer and the only white face in the room.

The hand that reached down to shake his was, he discovered, softer and smoother than Hattie's when she finished her toilette in the evening. The mouth smiling down at him was like a single straight line drawn with a ruler.

"Hello there, young man, we've all been waiting to get a look at you. Think you'll enjoy your stay with us?"

"Yes," he said.

"What's the weather like in the City of Light?" This to Hattie with the thin-lipped smile. "Rain, I imagine."

"What else?" Hattie said with a laugh. "It's March."

"I try to stay away from there this time of year."

"Oh, do you come over often?" she asked.

"Yes, I have friends and colleagues there." Turning abruptly back to him, the lawyer chucked him under the chin. "Enjoy yourself, young man."

Only one other face there stayed with him. He even remembered the name that went with it. Yusef Jordan. He was the young musical director for the concert and a piano player like his grandfather. The thing that struck him was that the Yusef Jordan man was wearing a kufi skullcap like the touts for the marabous back home. One look at the cap and the dark face under it and he caught himself asking the same question he secretly asked about the touts sometimes: whether his father looked anything like this man. His *sanspapiers* father who was rumored to have been a *vendeur* of picture postcards and mini Tour Eiffels to tourists on the steps of Sacré-Coeur. His father who had been caught and sent packing back to Africa.

This too he had overheard Hattie relate any number of times to Madame Molineaux.

Just as the balloon in his chest began to fill again, a hand came to rest on his shoulder and he was being drawn away

from both Hattie and all the people around them. His grandfather's brother, taking charge, was suddenly steering him
over to the office half of the room. There, saying he had
decided to rescue him, he put him to sit at his desk, first raising the desk chair so's he could reach it. He then slipped the
drawing *bloc* from under his arm and placed it in front of
him.

"I bet this comes in handy when you're around a lot of
grown folks talking their heads off."

How'd he guess?

The man winked at him and left.

"Man, Edgar, I still don't see how you got Abe Kaiser to sell
you that barn of his."

The final reports on the concert had been given, the
last-minute details cleared away, and they were all sitting
around having a drink and chatting, Shades Bowen dominating the conversation.

He had raised the subject of Putnam Royal where the
concert would be held and was talking mainly to Edgar
Payne.

"You must have worked some powerful roots on the cat."

Edgar Payne laughed. "No roots, no mojo, just some cre-
atively applied pressure which I left to Jerry here." He waved
toward his lawyer who gave a little bow, acknowledging his
role.

"Although old Abe doesn't seem to realize that he no
longer owns the place," Edgar Payne went on. "Every time
you look he's parked in his Caddy outside, acting like Putnam
Royal is still his."

"Putnam Plantation is more like it," Shades Bowen
rejoined. "That's how the son-of-a-b ran the club. You could

hardly ever get a contract outta him in the old days. And he was always coming up short with your money. Hattie can tell you. She had this girl group she was managing at the time used to play the Putnam too . . ."

He was seated on the sofa, Hattie at his side, and he turned to her. "What was the name of your group again? Cherisse with her pretty self was in it I remember."

"The Maconettes," she said. "We were all from around the block so we called ourselves the Maconettes."

"Yeah, that was it. You ever got a contract outta that man?"

"No."

"You ever got all the money he owed you?"

"Never."

"See what I mean!" This to Edgar Payne. "That was Abe for ya. So I'm glad, man, you bought him out, don't care how you had to do it.

"'Cause Putnam Royal really belongs to your brother!" he declared after a thoughtful pause. "He's the one put the place on the map. For a time, 'cause of him, it was almost as popular as some the big clubs in the City. Had folks from all over flocking to hear him. Had big-name musicians willing to come to Brooklyn to play there 'cause of him. Prez, Bud, Diz, Max, the masters. Putnam Royal woulda been nothing if not for Sonny-Rett Payne!"

"And it's where he got to be called Sonny-Rett." Hattie speaking. "Remember the Sunday that happened, Shades?"

"Girl, I never forgot!" Voice booming. "Sunday, the twelfth of October, the year of our Lord nineteen hundred and forty-seven. Tell 'em 'bout it, Hattie. You was the one closest to him back then. Give these young folks here a little history lesson."

Which she did. Garbed in her Parisian-chic, widow's-weeds black, strands of her graying sideburns peeking out from under the Sikh turban, her ordinary face with the extraordinary skin raised slightly, she reminisced for them.

"It was the first time he got a chance to sit in with the band," she said, "at something Abe Kaiser had started called Sunday Jazz at the Putnam Royal. And of all things, he decided to play some hokey-doke, Tin Pan Alley tune called 'Sonny Boy Blue' from a Broadway musical at the time. For some reason he chose that song, but from the moment he put his hands down on that piano, from the very first chord, it was 'Sonny Boy Blue' like it had never been played before."

"Cat put a hurtin' on it!" Shades Bowen.

"That tune," she said, "didn't have *nothing* to do with Tin Pan Alley or Broadway when he laid into it. We couldn't believe what we were hearing. Nobody we knew, certainly nobody from Brooklyn, had ever played piano like that. When he was done we all just sat there, dumbstruck. Remember, Shades?"

He nodded solemnly, eyes hidden behind the blind-man's glasses.

"Sat there," Hattie went on, "like we were in church and weren't supposed to clap. Everybody spellbound. Until Alvin Edwards, lived on Decatur Street, used to play trumpet till he got his arm blown off in the war—Alvin still alive, Shades?"

"Naw," he said. "Horse rode Alvin outta here years ago."

For a moment Hattie paid her respects, her head bowed in silence. Then: "Until Alvin jumped up all of a sudden and started shouting 'Sonny-Rett! Sonny-Rett! Sonny-Rett!' And pointing to him up on the bandstand with the hand he had left. Just shouting the new name he'd given him and pointing like he'd gone crazy!

"You weren't there." She turned sharply to Edgar Payne. "You didn't get to hear him." The edge to her voice again. "So lemme tell you. Your brother took that sappy little tune, put a hurtin' on it like Shades said, and made it his tune, his song. Alvin understood that and made it part of his name. Anyway, before you knew it, everybody was on their feet shouting Sonny-Rett and clapping. A standing ovation that just wouldn't quit. The guys in the band clapping. Abe Kaiser clapping. I tell you, old bucket-o'-blood Putnam Royal had never seen anything like it!"

"I were there!" Shades Bowen. His hand up. A witness.

Hattie also held up her hand. Another witness. "Naturally," she said, "Abe hired him on the spot. Made him the headliner on Sundays. Little goody-two-shoes Everett Payne—that's what we used to call him around the block when we were growing up, always in the house practicing—was suddenly Sonny-Rett Payne, the headliner at Sunday Jazz at the Royal . . ."

Hattie shook her head, remembering, reminiscing, amazed.

"How's it going?"

The man had materialized at his elbow.

"All right," he said. He was working on a drawbridge gate, modeling it on the dungeon-like basement gates on Macon Street.

"Hey, that looks familiar. You've got a good eye."

"Thanks," he said, although he wasn't sure what that meant.

"Can I get you some more soda?"

"No thanks."

He had treated him to a glass of ginger ale earlier. And

instead of sending someone with it, he had brought it over himself, along with a napkin for him to wipe his mouth and a coaster to protect the desk.

"You sure?"

"Yes."

"Okay," he said, leaving. "We should be finished soon."

Unlike the others busy talking talking talking, and that included Hattie (although she had stopped long enough to look over when he was being served the soda), Edgar Payne had not forgotten he was there.

You can call me simply Uncle Edgar he had said at the airport, but only when it feels right to you.

Meanwhile, the piano player/music director, Yusef Jordan in his kufi skullcap, had come over and taken a seat close to Hattie. He had listened almost reverently to her before, and now he had a proposal to put to her. Would she be willing to share with the audience at the concert some of her reminiscences of Sonny-Rett? Some of the stories and anecdotes she must remember from her long association with him. Especially things from all his years in Europe. What had it been like for him as a working musician over there, in the clubs, on the road, at recording sessions?

"The life stories behind the music," he said. "They would add so much to the memorial."

"I'm no storyteller," Hattie said flatly.

"You a lie!" Shades Bowen cried. "Girl, you the best! You ought've heard yourself just now."

Everyone agreed and Yusef Jordan, encouraged, continued to press her: "It would mean so much to those like myself who never knew him in person. I remember the first time I heard his recording of that old 'Sonny' tune. I was like you that Sunday back in forty-seven. I didn't know any-body could play piano like that. It blew me away. From then on he became my teacher. Never met him, was only a kid when he died, but he became my teacher.

"Love his work!" he declared passionately. "And it's not just me and other musicians and people who've admired him over the years, but a lot of the young people just get-ting into jazz. They've also discovered Sonny-Rett Payne. I hear them talking about him. A whole new generation. They'd love to learn more about his life. Please," he said, adding that the reminiscences would also be an ideal way to introduce the Sonny-Rett tunes the band would be playing. She could share with them a story or anecdote before each number . . .

"It's a wonderful idea," Edgar Payne said. He had been standing close by, listening intently. "And on a practical note we'd more than make it worth your while."

"Man's talking money, Hattie." Shades Bowen. "And talk-ing a contract too. All of us on this planning committee got contracts. This ain't no fly-by-night Abe Kaiser operation."

"Of course a contract. Jerry will see to that."

"I can have it ready tomorrow." The lawyer. His smile.

A fervent Yusef Jordan appeared about to kneel before her. "I can't tell you what it would mean for you to be part of the concert, Miss Carmichael. It would be such an honor."

"Let the church say amen!" Shades Bowen held up his drink.

The others followed suit, glasses held high.

"Wait a minute, wait a minute," Hattie cried, and she was all of a sudden laughing. "I haven't said yes yet! I haven't seen the contract!"

Hattie laughing? The sound brought his head up from the drawing *bloc*. He hadn't heard her laugh, really laugh, since they arrived in this place called Brooklyn.

7

"Pourquoi?"

As he curled into sleep, still warm from the man's arms that had half-carried him up the stairs (he'd been too sleepy to climb on his own), he heard Hattie in the living room asking *"Pourquoi?"* and all the laughter was gone from her voice.

"Pourquoi? You were never any fan of your brother's. So why this big concert all of a sudden? Why all the records?"

A wave toward the scores of Sonny-Rett albums and CDs surrounding the huge, state-of-the-art stereo.

"You've been waiting to ask that since you arrived, haven't you."

"Before that," she said. "Ever since your letter turned up on my doorstep."

Edgar Payne was about to leave when her question stopped him, and with a thin, resigned smile that said he had been expecting it, he had turned back and gone to sit in the lounge chair. He still had on his coat, but had removed his hat. The moment he took it off, all the light in the room had flocked like so many birds to nest on the bald dome of his head.

"You're right," he admitted. "I was no fan of his. For the longest time I didn't understand his kind of music, didn't like it, and above all didn't want anything to do with it given the grief it caused when we were growing up. That most of all. I held that against him for the longest time."

He spoke without apology.

"Then one night, not long after we heard he had died, I turned on the radio as I was driving home and there he was. Some jazz station out of Newark was featuring his music in an all-night tribute to him. Practically the entire show devoted to him. And maybe because he was dead and what I felt about him or his music really didn't matter anymore, I didn't switch stations and actually forced myself to listen . . ."

"And?" Hattie was seated across from him on the sofa. A coffee table lay between them and a good five feet of floor space.

"And after a while I found I wasn't forcing myself anymore. I was listening because I wanted to. And I wanted to keep on listening, so that when the station's signal began to fade, I turned around and drove back to Brooklyn and spent the rest of the night in this chair listening until the station signed off. The next day I went out and bought every record of his I could lay my hands on, which wasn't many, and from then on started slowly building the collection you see here—it took years—and slowly began educating myself in the music of one Sonny-Rett Payne, my kid brother, after refusing to listen to him for decades."

"So the concert is about making it up to him, right?"

There it was again: the barbed edge to her voice Hattie couldn't help.

"I suppose you could look at it that way." Edgar Payne disregarded her tone. "But it's also about bringing him home in a manner of speaking and ending his anger with us and this place."

"He had a right to be angry!"

"You think I don't know that?" He spoke quietly. "I lived in that house with the two of them, remember. I can still hear to this day the sound of the strap the times Ulene caught him playing what he wasn't supposed to be playing or spotted him hanging out in that record store where you worked listening to what he wasn't supposed to be listening to . . ."

Hattie remembered: Birdell's on Reid Avenue and thirteen-, fourteen-year-old Everett Payne, wearing knickers and argyle kneesocks, on his way home from piano lessons, the music of Bach, Beethoven, Schubert, et al. under his arm. He would slip into Birdell's to listen on the sly to Tatum, Basie, Muddy Waters, et al. He always left the records in a mess for her to put back in their jackets. She didn't mind. Besides, that was part of her job.

"Your mother came storming in the store one day and saw us talking, just talking about a record, and she cursed me out like I was to blame for him being there!"

"Cause for another beating when she got him home, I'm sure." Edgar Payne shook his head, sorrowing. "Me, I used to run and cover my ears, but there was no escaping the sound of that strap. And that was all you heard, because my brother never uttered a word, never cried, never begged her to stop. He just stood there and took it . . ."

A reflective pause, then: "It was like he already understood, young as he was, that the strap in one form or another was the price he might always have to pay for playing what he wanted to. And he accepted it.

"Me," he repeated, "all I wanted was for him to stop

aggravating her so there'd be some peace in the house. I blamed him for all the unhappiness around there. I can't tell you how glad I was when he turned seventeen, upped his age, and joined the army."

An even longer pause, then an abrupt reversal, sudden guilt and remorse in his voice and in the hooded eyes: "I should have helped him, I know. I could have kept a look-out and warned him when I saw her coming so he could switch back to what she wanted to hear. I never did that. After the beatings I could have at least said something to let him know that I felt for him. We were never close, but I could have tried to understand him and to protect him . . ."

"You were the oldest!" Hattie sharply reminded him.

He nodded. "People like him need protection. Personally, I wouldn't have wanted his life, as wonderful as it must have been for a time. I don't mind being a Dutch burgher whose only talent is buying and selling. But once I opened up to his music, really started listening to it, I slowly began to understand *his* way, his art, his life, and to respect it, even admire it, simple burgher that I am."

A little self-deprecating shrug. "You know what that means?"

"Of course I do! I'm no dummy!"

"That's what Everett used to call me, y'know. A Dutch burgher. He must have read it somewhere. He had no use for my kind.

"As for Ulene?" he went on. "Another story. He broke her heart with that music of his, then broke it again when he disappeared for good over in Europe. Never a word from him! As hard as she worked to pay for those lessons of his. It's hard to forgive him for that.

"And yet"—a bitter laugh—"whose picture does she keep on top of the piano? Certainly not mine."

Edgar Payne reached for his hat and rose heavily to his feet. "It's time I made tracks for Long Island."

"Another question." Hattie wasn't through with him yet. "How'd you find me?"

"You've been waiting to ask that too, haven't you?"

"*How?*"

"That's an even longer story. Let's leave it for another time, okay? What's important is that we found you and you agreed to come and you brought my brother's grandson with you."

He stood over by the door, hat on, looking suddenly weary, a man weighted down, it appeared, by something even more troubling that needed to be said.

Cautiously: "Tell me, would you ever consider coming back here to live?"

An incredulous look from the sofa, then Hattie was drawing herself up proudly. "I'll have you know, monsieur, that I already have my plot, bought and paid for, next to theirs in Cimetière de Montmartre. Do I have to translate that for you?"

"No," he said and left, shoulders still bowed under the thing that remained unsaid.

8

*"I went to my father and I said
'Papa, the white people war finish,
give me my passage and my show money.'"*

Like an importunate suitor, Edgar Payne was back early the next day. His mother, he said, had telephoned him shortly after he arrived at the office to demand that he bring "the boychild" to visit her forthwith.

"Ulene giving orders again. And of course there's no saying no to her." This to Hattie with a resigned sigh. If it was all right with her, this time he would walk Sonny over to the house and pick him up afterward, that way sparing her any further unpleasantness.

The venomous cut-eye. Hattie agreed.

Sonny quickly put away his drawing *bloc* and went and got his coat.

The piano! He would get to play it again!

Outside, late March had done a predictable about-face, so that the day which greeted them as they stepped onto Macon Street was almost spring-like—more blue than gray to the sky, a warmer sun, and a wind that had downgraded itself to a mild breeze.

The moment they were out of Hattie's sight, had she been watching them from the window, Edgar Payne stopped, bent down, and, giving him a conspiratorial wink, began unbuttoning his coat. He himself was without coat, hat, scarf, and gloves, and now he was boldly unbuttoning Sonny's coat that Hattie had insisted, just minutes ago, had to be buttoned all the way up to the neck.

Pneumonia weather she had called the sudden spring-like day.

"Don't tell, okay."

"Okay," he said and to prove that he could be equally as bold out of Hattie's sight, he stripped off his gloves and stuffed them in his pocket and snatched the hat off his head.

This earned him the little playful uppercut that scarcely grazed his chin. It was the second one so far.

They resumed walking.

"What's the writing on your ring say?"

He decided he would take advantage of the boldness he felt while it lasted.

The man immediately stopped again and began working the outsize ring off his finger. He placed it, a laird's royal seal, into the palm of his hand.

The heft of it!

"It's Latin," he said. "It tells the name of the college I went to which was right here in Brooklyn and the date it was founded. And that's the seal of the school on top. You know what a seal is?"

"Yes."

"That's right, you would," he laughed. "What with all your King Arthur castles. Anyway, this is what's called a class ring. You can buy one when you graduate to have as a souvenir of your college days."

He didn't know if they had the custom in France, but if they did he would have a ring like it when he graduated from college. He'd like that, wouldn't he?

He started to say yes, only to remind himself that it would depend on whether Hattie had been able to put her hands on some real money by then. So instead of saying yes, he shrugged and started to give back the ring.

"No, hold on to it till we reach the house."

The ring in his closed palm, he almost heard himself saying "uncle" in his head . . .

To reach the house, No. 301, they had to cross Macon Street and walk more than halfway up the long block. With the rush hour over the street was almost deserted and practically the only sound, aside from that of the passing cars, was the work being done on the houses under repair, including the one where Hattie once lived. The hard hats of the men working aloft the scaffolding were a brighter, more vivid yellow than the sun.

"My grandnephew, fellas, visiting us from Paris for the first time!" Edgar Payne occasionally stopped to introduce him to the workers on the lower level of the scaffolds. "He speaks French naturally, but he also speaks English like he was born right here on Macon Street. He's come to see what life is like over this way. We're hoping he likes it."

Showing him off like he was a *vedette,* a movie star.

The great-grandmother woman looked the same as when he'd met her two days ago. Her tall, stern figure appeared at the basement gate in the same stained housedress and misbuttoned coat-like sweater, her hair uncombed under her ugly hat, and the hand it was hard not to stare at doing its trembly dance at her side.

"Well, here he is as ordered, Ma. Your great-grand come to visit you again."

"I see him." Her clouded gaze had immediately attached itself to his face through the bars of the gate.

"Can I come in and do anything for you before I leave?"

"Not a thing. I can still do for myself I'll have you know."

"Any groceries you need?"

An impatient suck-teeth. "I has already called down to the store and ordered everything I need."

She was treating the man no better, Sonny decided, than she had Hattie. And as with Hattie, she clearly had no intention of opening the gate while he remained in the yard.

"All right, Ma," Edgar Payne said, voice pained, despairing yet loving. The dutiful son. "I'll be back for him in an hour. You two have a good time."

The moment he stepped out of the yard, she unlocked the dungeon gate, a version of which was in his drawing *bloc,* and he stepped inside.

As with the first visit, she hurried him through the stale, entombed mustiness of the basement and up the walled-in, dark-as-midnight stairway (where she had yelled at him) that led to the parlor floor. Her speeded-up shuffle took them under the rusted sprinkler pipes in the hallway and over the runner turning to dust underfoot, until they reached the stairway to the two upper floors. Then, the abrupt halt and, livid, her voice charging up the dark stairs: "Turn off the lights and the blasted radios up there! You think I own Con Edison? Damn roomers! You's more trouble than profit!"

He hadn't told on her about yelling at persons unseen.

The next minute, she was sending the double doors on the other side of the hall rumbling magically out of sight and leading him through the packed warehouse of shabby mismatched furniture that was her living room.

It stood ready and waiting for him, the old upright with the picture of his grandfather as a boy on top. She had already uncovered the keyboard and opened the panels in the high front, exposing the long, perforated roll of paper inside—it still looked to him like *papier hygiénique*—that somehow, magically, created the music.

This time he was left on his own from the beginning. The moment he sat on the bench, the woman pressed the switch at the end of the keyboard and then went and sat in the overstuffed armchair that might have been used as a feline scratching post. The music promptly soared before she even left his side, and just as promptly he began chasing down the keys rising and falling on either side of middle C, playing the game as she had taught him.

"All right, you's to rest yourself."

He was starting the entire roll again when she called over to him.

"I'm not tired," he said and kept at the chase, missing most of the keys as usual, but having fun anyway.

"I said stop, turn off the piano and rest yourself."

Her tone! He quickly did as he was ordered. He even covered the keyboard and closed the panels over the piano roll after pressing the switch to "off."

He ended up spending the rest of the visit seated next to her on a frayed and lumpy sofa, the springs gone, looking at a single small snapshot in a dog-eared photograph album she unearthed from the chaos in the room.

The snapshot, old and badly faded, showed two young women in long, pale, old-timey dresses and wide-brimmed summer hats, posing on a dock somewhere, the black hull of a ship behind them. The taller and darker of the two had a large suitcase at her side that was shaped exactly like a doctor's bag, and they were both holding on tightly to identical fringed "flapper" handbags.

"You know who the body is?" Pointing to the one with the odd-looking suitcase at her side.

Body? She must mean "person."

"You?" He took a guess.

She nodded; then a proud boast: "I came to this man country with nothing but a gripsack and two willing hands!"

She held them out for him to see, large, work-worn, and a lesser shade of brownish-black than his own, the left one fluttering as if it were a leaf in the mild breeze outside.

"And who this is?" Pointing to the other woman, who was small-built and lighter-skinned, hers a shy, hopeful smile under the wide brim of her hat.

"I don't know."

"How you mean you don't know!" A sudden outburst. "You ain' got eyes in yuh head? You can't see it's Alva."

Her mind isn't what it used to be, he had heard the man say to Hattie. Later, when he asked her what that meant, she'd said, "Oh, her mind probably comes and goes sometimes like a lot of old people." Maybe, he thought, it was like the on-and-off switch on her piano, her mind. He bent his head, folded his hands in his lap. There was nothing to do then but wait until it switched back to normal. Or the hour visit was over.

"Alva! Alva! We was friends from small. How you mean you don't know who she is!"

Her overturned gaze on his bent head.

*　　　*　　　*

How could he not know Alva, who had lived down the road from her in Carlton Village from the time they was small. The two of them was like twins, people said, 'cause they did everything together. Had been christened as babies together at the Anglican church, then later confirmed there together, both of them wearing pretty white frocks and a bride's veil on their heads. God's brides. Had been schoolgirls together from primer standard on. And dreamers together. Dreaming, both of them, of leaving the little miserable two-by-four island for big America soon as the war finish—the white people at the time gassing and killing each other and calling it a world war never mind is only them fighting. And Alva with a big sister already gone to live in a place called Brooklyn and ready and willing to receive them and help them find work. And the two of them having to wait. 1918. The damn war finish. The white people tired killing each other for a time. And soon as it finish she and Alva booked passage. The SS *Nerissa*. An old tub been down here since they said "Come let us make boats." And the sea hard. Her and Alva puking and praying, praying and puking the whole time and bawling like babies for their mothers. All the same, they reached safe and the minute they set foot in New York there was Alva big sister with a box camera to take their picture.

"I came to this man country with nothing but a gripsack and two willing hands. You hear me?"

Sonny nodded. It was best to simply nod.

And Alva sister didn't waste no time finding them work. They wasn't in the country no time before she had them sleeping-in jobs in someplace call Long Island. The work hard. Her one cleaning a big ten-room house, her one cooking, her one caring for the children as well as an old fretful grandmother that lived with them. The woman always acting like she smell something bad the minute you come near her when is she the one messing herself. The work hard and only every other Thursday and one Sunday a month off. But never mind. I seeing green in my hand, she told herself, and green in the new bank book. Then, four years into the sleep-in, on one of her Sundays off, which she always spent at Alva sister house in Brooklyn she met up with one Bertram Payne. Nothing to look at and he had a good few years on him, but he was from Home and was a serious somebody with a good job at a mattress factory and his own little business on the weekend going about selling hair grease, hot combs, creams 'n' such you couldn't find in the stores if you was Colored. That's what he was doing at Alva sister house that Sunday. Selling. A man she could tell right off wasn't frighten for work. And he could tell the same about her.

Alva stood up with her at the wedding down to City Hall. Alva as godmother to Edgar DeCorsey, her first. Alva at her side four years later when she almost died having the second one, Everett Carlyle, who would be her heart and later the ruination of her heart. And her good friend from small was at her side again when Bertram Payne suddenly passed. A man never sick a day in his life and then one night in his sleep a stroke. They said it was a stroke. You wake the morning to find the man dead next to you in the bed. And the house on Macon Street the two of you just start to buy to be paid for, the mortgage they had to get from a loan shark when the banks refuse them being they was Colored, higher—three, four times higher—than any bank's.

And two boychildren to raise her one.

And times hard after that idiot Hoover near-ruined the

country. Rich people turned poor overnight throwing them-
self out the windows 'cause they don' know how to cut-and-
contrive. That's what you must do, y'know, when times is
hard. Is what she, Ulene Agatha Payne, born Cummings,
Mis' Cummings' girlchild, did right away: cut-and-contrive.
First, with the little insurance money Bertram Payne left she
changed over Mr. House into rooms: dining room into bedroom, sprinkler pipe from bottom to top. Second, she went
back down on the white people floor. Day's work this time.
Three, four days a week found her one in a mob looking for
work all the way out in Flatbush, the mob of them gathered
under the Franklin Avenue El at Albemarle Road, hoping to
land a job for a day. West Indian and American alike—
everybody catching it but a hundred times worse if you
black—crowd together, sheltering from the rain, hot sun, and
snow under the stairs to the El at Albemarle Road and waiting to dash out in the road the minute a car with a Madam at
the wheel start to pull over. The Madams Jew and Gentile,
Gentile and Jew, but mostly Jew what with them taking over
Flatbush and the Gentile running from them out to Long
Island. And all of them running from us. A country where
everybody always running from the next body feeling they's
better. But mark my words, one these days they gon all run
out of where-to-run.

The minute a car pull up she was nearly always the first
at the driver-side window, willing to work for even a half-
day if nothing else. And windows? Do you do windows?
Yes, Madam, I does windows.

Times hard. Everybody catching it. Even the American
woman across the street at Two fifty-eight who gets on like
she own Macon Street turned up under the El. Her husband
all of a sudden leave her. He get fed up, people say, with her

treating him like he was nothing but a paycheck and leave. Every penny the man made went on her back, on the back of the spoil-rotten little girl she has and on the house her father dead and leave her, that she's turned into a palace. And with the husband gone and plenty bills to pay, she had to find herself under the El with the rest of us. But if you see how the woman come dress to do day's work! In a coat with fur on the collar and cuffs. And hat, shoes, and gloves that you can see cost more than what the Madams-them wearing! Who's gon hire somebody dress better than them? That looks like she came to hire them to clean *her* house!

The foolish woman din' know it, but she was gon have to learn how to cut-and-contrive like herself. For an example, when the Madams gave her their old t'row-off clothes and furnitures she kept what was halfway decent for herself—like the old player piano one of them gave her—and sold the rest. Her living room was full of t'row-off furnitures to sell. Another thing: in Moore Street market is only the five cents a pound blue-back kosher chickens she's buying, the cheapest. Chickens so old that when you plucked them the skin on the backs showed blue from the deep roots of the feathers. And day-old Tastee bread from Ward's outlet bakery, the price cut in half. Meatballs that when she made them was more bread than meat. It was cut-and-contrive down to the very toilet paper. Her children knew that if they didn't want to feel the strap they was not to throw out the wrapping paper on a new roll. They was to use the wrapping paper first.

And day and night she had to be after the disgusting roomers running up the electric bill with the lights, the radios.

All that to meet the loan shark mortgage each month and to pay for Everett's lessons.

I tell yuh, your middle name is cut-and-contrive, Alva used to say to her all the time.

Alva. Oh God, Alva. Her good good friend from small. She and all ended up under the El at Albemarle Road. When you hear the shout she lose the good, steady sleep-in job she had. Was foolish enough to let the Madam husband have his way with her till she find herself making feet for stockings—and lose the job. Alva bringing a child into this world that looked everything like a little white mice. The shame of it. Alva forced to do common day's work with the rest of us. Alva living with the child in a cold-water railroad flat on Reid Avenue you could run a rat through. Her chances finish.

"Ulene, as God is my witness, I regret the day I set foot in this man country."

And don't you know she let the regretfulness and shame eat away at her till she get a cancer that put her in her grave before her time. Her friend from small gone!

But not her! Not Ulene! She never once regretted having gone to her father the day the war finish . . .

"I went to my father and I said 'Papa, the white people war finish, give me my passage and my show money.' "

The woman turned to Sonny with this on the lumpy, t'row-off sofa, startling him—she had been quiet for such a long time.

"And I know," she said, "my father went straight and sell off part of his cane-piece and put the money in my hand."

"Show money?" He had perked up at that. "What show didja go see?"

When Hattie finally decided to accept the money the man had sent, she had splurged and taken him to a show at one of the cinemas at Odéon, across the river near Paree Cinq.

"What show? What show?" she asked, staring bewilderedly at him. Then another outburst: "But you's an igno-ramus or what!? The show money, I'll have you know, was fifty big U.S. dollars you had to show to the authorities here the minute you stepped off the boat to prove you wasn't coming to be a pauper in their country. How it 'tis you don' know that?"

He shrugged. It was best to simply shrug and lower his head again.

Silence, except for her raveled breathing and, from out-side, the sound of the work crews, although this was almost muffled into silence by the tightly closed, faded winter drapes at the windows and the mass of stationary dust motes that suffused the air.

Until: "But Ulene, how could the child know somethin' like that?" Her mind finally switching on again. "He's gon think you's a madwoman."

She turned to him on the sofa. "You wish somethin' to drink?"

She asked so humbly that he said yes, but only after making her wait a good few seconds.

The kitchen which was at the rear of the basement down-stairs and looked out onto the backyard would have had the same effect on Hattie as did Madame Molineaux's apart-ment. It would have turned her stomach. Had she seen it, she would have strictly forbidden him to eat or drink any-thing there.

At the thought of her admonition, he kept his eyes closed as he drank the orange juice the woman gave him, so as not to see the smudged glass in his hand (had it been washed?) or the condition of the room.

9

"Hattie's not old!"

"What's the name again of the lady in the picture on your desk? The one who's your wife."

The visit over, he and the man were on their way back up Macon Street, the midday sun high above the brownstones, the work crews on the block gone to lunch, their hammers and other tools silenced.

"Alva. That's your great-aunt Alva. You'll meet her on Friday. Why'd you ask?"

"Your mother showed me a picture of herself long ago and a lady with the same name."

"Ah, I know the picture. That's my wife's mother who was also my godmother."

"She yelled at me because I didn't know who it was."

Telling on her finally. But she had gone too far this time. Calling him an ignoramus!

Edgar Payne: "Oh, no, I'm sorry. I apologize for her. It's that she gets so confused sometimes. Did she upset you?"

"No. My *nounou* sometimes yells at me too."

"Your *nounou*?"

"My sitter, Madame Molineaux. She lives on our floor. She minds me when Hattie's at work."

Some nights, once Hattie put him to bed and left for the Club Violette, Madame Molineaux would slip into his room, not to check on him—it would be too soon for that—but simply looking for company.

His was the smaller of the apartment's two cramped rooms, a bedroom scarcely bigger than a closet with a warped door that didn't close flush and one small, high window from which nothing was to be seen except a blank square of sky. It had been the runaway's bedroom. His girl-mother. What had she daydreamed about looking up at the one empty window? The other, larger room was a living and dining room combined, and the place where he did his homework, his drawing, and where he and Madame Molineaux—without Hattie knowing—sometimes sat up late on Friday and Saturday nights playing one of the donated secondhand games he borrowed from St.-Joseph-des-Epinettes. Monopoly was their favorite. During the day, the room served as Hattie's bedroom. While he was at school, she slept there on the sofa bed, surrounded by pictures of his grandfather and his *vedette* grandmother.

She had as many pictures of one as she did of the other.

Even on weeknights, Madame Molineaux would sometimes come sit with him as soon as Hattie left. A healthy shot of Père Magloire in hand, she would deposit her arthritic bones on the side of his bed, her head with its steady *non, non, non* seemingly denying every cruel word that issued from her mouth.

That's what Hattie had told Sonny the tic meant. She once explained that the nonstop "no" of Madame Molineaux's head proved she didn't mean the things she said about the Algerians. These were things he was never to believe or to say himself. With some people, especially when they reached a certain age, part of them, the good part, couldn't always control the bad things other parts of them were saying or doing. That was the case with his *nounou,* according to Hattie. What he must do, then, was to pay attention to her head, her good part, and not to what came out of her mouth. That way he could still love her.

Occasionally, with her seated on his bed airing her usual litany, he'd fall asleep, and once in a while she'd yell.

It had happened only last month.

"*M'sieur!*"

"*Oui?*" His eyes had flown open. He had sat up like a sprung jack-in-the-box.

"You're not listening to me!" Madame Molineaux in her working-class argot.

"*Pas vrai! J'écoute, j'écoute!* Not so! I'm listening!"

"*Tu mens, toi!* You're lying!"

"*Pas vrai!*" he repeated, his voice as sharp.

He was annoyed at being awakened. He'd been slipping into a dream, a happy one tonight, and not the nightmare that still sometimes awaited him in sleep; the one about his namesake grandfather, in which he heard his screams in the empty Châtelet station of the Métro where he had died, heard also his long brutal fall down the endless flight of concrete stairs, but although he—Sonny—went running and searching and calling for him everywhere in the huge station he couldn't find him, couldn't rescue him . . .

It was a dream drawn from the talk he overheard the nights Hattie painfully reminisced, thinking Madame Molineaux was her sole audience. True, she told him the good parts about his grandfather and the others all the time. But there were things, she said, many things she would tell him only when he was old enough. These were the things he had to strain his ears to overhear when he was supposed to be sleeping, the talk reaching him through the pencil-thin opening in the warped bedroom door.

In the happy dream that had just begun to unfold when he was jarred awake, he was over at Jean-Jacques' house where there was a *télé*. And he and his best friend from school weren't only watching it, they were inside it, on the screen, the two of them changed into a pair of knights astride their mounts, on their way to an adventure somewhere.

"Okay then, m'sieur, tell me what I was talking about?"

"*Les Algériens, quoi!* The Algerians, what else!"

"*Non!*"

"*Le quartier.*"

"*Non! Tu as des yeux, mais tu ne vois rien!* You have eyes but you don't see anything! And you've completely forgotten what today is. *Tu ne m'aimes pas!* You don't love me!"

Hurt. She was clearly hurt.

It was then that he sleepily noticed that she was wearing her good dress. Instead of the untidy shifts she usually wore, she had put on the dress she reserved for the first of the month when she went to collect her pension check at the *bureau de poste* nearby. (She had been a shopgirl for years in a neighborhood dry goods and notions store that had closed down when the *quartier* changed.) Accompanied by Hattie, she disdainfully hobbled the short distance to the post office. After cashing the check, the first francs went to Père Magloire. First things first. The rest she handed over to Hattie who, in exchange for her looking after him, paid her bills and did all her shopping.

Her good dress. Apart from the first of the month, the

only other time she wore it was on the birthday of the soldier who had been the love of her long-ago young life. Monsieur Molineaux, the husband of her later years, now dead, could never compare she said to her foot soldier who had fought and died for la belle France in Indochina decades ago. She kept a picture of him in her bedroom, framed on one side by a miniature flag of Mali (he had been from Francophone black Africa), and on the other by a smaller version of the large tricolor hanging above her front door.

Today was the foot soldier's *anniversaire* and he, Sonny, had failed to notice that she was wearing her good dress in memory of him; worse, he had fallen asleep just as she began telling him of their life together—all the good times!—when her love was on leave in Paris. Hurt, she had yelled.

Never mind, she soon forgave him and, taking his fore-finger, she dipped it, only the very tip of it, into her glass. A single drop of Père Magloire for him to place on his tongue, so that he could toast along with her *le grand amour* of her youth.

"And what's she like, this sitter who yells at you some-times?" Edgar Payne was asking.

Quickly Sonny reminded himself of what he was not to mention about her and safely said, "She only goes out once a month. She's too old she says to be climbing up and down six flights of stairs."

"You're around old people a lot, aren't you?"

"Hattie's not old!"

Whenever he caught her without her Sikh turban on and saw the thin, patchy gray that scarcely covered her head, he would feel the balloon in his chest begin to fill, ready to stifle his breathing, his heart, and to bring on the floodgate.

"She's not!" Almost shouting.

"Of course not, of course not, I didn't mean Hattie," Edgar Payne said hastily. To reassure him of this, he reached out to touch the small shoulder beside him. But his hand missed, because Sonny, angry with the man for the first time, had speeded up and was hurrying ahead up Macon Street.

And to think he had been close to calling him Uncle!

10

*"Glad to be here, God, with the use
and activity of these limbs and clothed
in my rightful mind. Amen."*

On the same sidewalk the following day, Thursday, on the way to No. 258 at the opposite end of the block, Hattie suddenly came to a halt as a large, light green passenger van marked "Landmark Conservancy Tours" drove past them. All along she had been walking as if taking two steps back for every reluctant one she took forward, and now she stopped walking altogether.

Sonny stopped also, looked up at her, and waited. And waited.

"You know," she said finally, her gaze on the van which had had time to pull over and park in front of the house in the distance, "I really should spend this morning thinking about what I'm supposed to do at the concert. I'm not sure what I'm getting myself into . . ."

Late yesterday afternoon, over in Edgar Payne's office, she had signed the contract his lawyer had drawn up for her. She had put on a small show of dissatisfaction in signing it, as if the money being offered was far less than what she'd expected, and she was only grudgingly accepting it. When she and Sonny were back at the house, though, she had let out a whoop.

"Things are beginning to look up on this trip," she'd said and, waving the cashier's check which was for half of the amount, she had whooped again.

"So would you mind," she asked, "if I didn't go with you on the visit this morning?"

"No," he said, although he did mind.

"You sure?"

"Yes."

"I know all about that so-called tour guide talk she gives. So does everybody who grew up on this block. Just tell her I had to attend to something about the concert and couldn't make it, okay?"

"Okay."

She would stand and watch him, she said, until he was safely inside the house. And she'd come pick him up the minute he phoned. He knew the number by now, didn't he?

"Yes," he said and rattled it off for her.

"My big fella! My savior!" She bussed him *à la française* on either cheek. "*A tout à l'heure!*"

"*Oui.*"

He set off on his own up the block, trying to walk as if he didn't mind her absence, and checking every so often over his shoulder to make sure she was there. Each time he looked back she blew him a kiss.

By the time he reached 258, the vanload of people were already assembled in the yard, over near the tree with the plaque on its trunk. There were about ten in all, mostly older men and women with silvery-white hair far whiter than their faces and dressed in plain, practical clothes and comfortable shoes. But no coats. It was another spring-like day. They were gathered around the guide, a lively, freckled-face young woman in a jacket the same light, spring green as the van. She was pointing out the plaque and the tree's summer foliage and talking talking talking.

He slipped past them up the high stoop, gave a glance back at Hattie—she was still there—and the minute he rang the bell found himself facing the large live-in maid the City supplied. Dora. Today she had on an even frillier little apron and cap.

"Mis' McCullum been waitin' on you."

He quickly ducked inside.

The great-grandmother woman he was to call by her rightful name, Florence Varina, and who despite her meanness he had found it in his heart to forgive, sat waiting for him on the camelback sofa that was positioned like a throne at the front of her *palais royal* living room.

At her side stood a small occasional table with a single drawer and the delicate, skittish legs of a foal.

"My baby's grandbaby!" Frail bony arms opened wide. Her wonderful toilette smell. He hugged her back, suddenly glad to see her and her pretty house.

"You got here just in time," she said. "'Cause I want you right next to me when those folks in the yard come upstairs."

She patted the place beside her and he sat down.

He was on one side of her, the antique table on the other.

"Where's that Hattie?"

"She said she had to attend to something about the concert."

She fanned this down. "She couldn't think of a better excuse? Well, never mind her. So long as you're here I'm happy. And look at you, all dressed up again!" (It was yet another suit from the shopping spree.) "You're a real classy gentleman just like my daddy. He was a man knew how to dress." She drew him close.

Shortly afterward the visitors filed in and were presented to her by the guide—the young woman treating Florence Varina as if she were, indeed, a royal personage. She, in turn, presented him.

"My great-grandson visiting from Paris, France. He lives in Paris, France. Was even born there. Speaks two languages."

Showing him off as the man had done yesterday. He didn't mind. In fact, he liked it.

To accommodate the group, who were introduced as members of the New England branch of the Conservancy, the occasional chairs in the room had been arranged in two rows facing the sofa, with an apron of empty floor space as in a theater in between.

Florence Varina gave them time to settle themselves and to appraise her and their surroundings. Herself first, her russet-dyed hair, her cover girl makeup, her earrings and choker, and the even more elaborate at-home gown, almost a ball gown, she had on today. A pair of high-heeled mules in the same fabric as the gown peeked out from under the long skirt.

An old-miss-young, Ulene Payne across the street called her.

The visitors were also given ample time to inspect her chandeliered, antiqued, mirrored, and marbled living room. "Welcome to my home," she had said to each of them during the introductions.

Finally she began. " 'Magnolia Grandiflora. Origin: Varina, Georgia. Planted April nine, eighteen eighty-nine, by

Mr. Gayton C. McCullum.' Did I get it right? That's what's on the plaque on that tree in my front yard, isn't it? I haven't been down there in a while to check on it. I'm like that Duke Ellington song: 'Don't Get Around Much Anymore.' "

The guide laughed, used to the joke, and the others followed.

"That plaque," she said, "gives you the basic facts about Miss Grandiflora, or Miss G. as I call her—her official name, when she was put in the ground, who placed her there, and such. So that's taken care of. And you've seen for yourself that she's no made-up, make-believe storybook tree, but the real one that grows in Brooklyn."

They laughed again.

"And I know that nice Miss Farrell here"—a smile in the direction of the guide—"has already told you all the botanical facts about Miss G. How tall she's supposed to grow, what time of year she shows off her big, pretty flowers, why she stays green like it's summer all year round. Who her relatives are. All such as that. Her scientific pedigree, in other words. That's Miss Farrell's department."

What she intended doing on the other hand, she went on to say, was to share with them Miss Grandiflora's personal story: why, for example, she decided to leave Varina, Georgia; the means by which she traveled all the way to Brooklyn, and the miracle of her survival for close to a hundred years in the cold, cold north.

"'Cause I'm sure you know Miss Grandiflora is strictly a southern lady."

During the laughter, she turned to the small table beside her, opened the single drawer under the top, and in the silence that fell once the laughter died, she began removing a number of items. First came a dresser scarf of beautiful

Battenberg lace. This she spread like an altar cloth on the table's bare surface. A cigar box followed—the thing as old and fragile as herself. She gently placed it on the pretty scarf. After this came a large, worn family Bible that was clearly older than both her and the cigar box. The last item was an expertly restored sepia photograph of a short, strongly built, dark-skinned man in a frock coat and spats, who stood squarely confronting the world beyond the picture frame with a pair of eyes that slanted slightly upward at the corners.

The picture went to the center of the display.

This done, Florence Varina resumed her talk. And now there was a noticeable change in her demeanor. Her playful air was gone. The unconscious preening she did to call attention to herself—fussing with her hair, her earrings, her choker, and the at-home gown—all that ceased. Also, what seemed another face—serious, even solemn, and altogether different from her usual one—emerged from the camouflage makeup.

"Mr. Gayton C. McCullum, my daddy." A worshipful bow toward the centerpiece photograph. "And the one responsible for Miss Grandiflora being here. To tell you her story like I promised I have to tell his too, if you don't mind. Well, he found, my daddy, that he had to leave Varina, Georgia, his home, and move his family north. Not that he wanted to. But he had no choice in the matter. And the one thing he decided to take with him when he left was Miss G. Why? You have to ask why he would bother taking a tree of all things, especially one that wasn't suited to the place where he was going."

She waited, then provided the answer herself: "As a remembrance. Miss G. would be something that would help him remember. He'd look out at her growing in his front yard in Brooklyn and right away call to mind Varina where he was born and had lived for upwards of fifty years and where he had looked forward to living until he died and could be buried on his own land."

His own land. She repeated this. Because Varina, she informed them, was in the only county in Georgia at the time where Colored were allowed to own land. And Mr. Gayton C. McCullum was one of the few that owned some, and out of those few he was the one doing the best. He was what you might even call a gentleman farmer. Had good land that he was always adding to. Had help working for him. Was head deacon in his church. An officer in the O. V. Catto Lodge of the Elks. He was somebody "high" amongst the Colored in Varina!

"Naturally, *certain* folks didn't take kindly to this. A Colored man living better than some of them. A Colored man owning good rich land. A Colored man trying to progress. For years they did all kinda meanness to aggravate his spirit and to hamper him in every way. It went on for years. Until finally one night he came home from a big lodge meeting up in Savannah to find his dogs poisoned, his help run off the place, the curing shed for his tobacco burned to the ground, and his wife and children hiding for their lives out in the woods . . .

"And the *certain* folks that did all that let it be known they weren't finished yet. His house and anybody in it would be next if he didn't sell and git. 'Cause it was his land they were after. And they would do it he knew, 'cause that was the beginning of the Jim Crow time when they were getting back at the Colored all over the South for having been freed.

"So my daddy sold. What else could he do? He wrote to his lodge and to his sister church in Brooklyn, told them to find him a house up there, and he sold. And his last day in

Varina he got up early that morning, gave thanks: 'Glad to be here, God, with the use and activity of these limbs and clothed in my rightful mind. Amen,' which is what he said every morning; he then put on that frock coat you see in the picture—he was a man loved to dress!—and all dressed up he went outside and began searching the ground under the magnolia tree he had out front. Just bent over searching and searching in his good clothes until he came across what he must have felt was the right piece of fruit fallen from the tree, the one that would help him to remember."

Here she picked up the cigar box as old as herself. "This is how Miss Grandiflora made the trip north."

Opening it, she removed a wax replica of the dark, cone-shaped fruit and held it up. "Looks like the real thing, doesn't it? The Conservancy had it made specially for me. And looks just like a grenade, doesn't it?" She made as if to lob it through the air, her first bit of playfulness since she began her talk.

To Sonny's surprise, she placed the piece of fake fruit in his hand.

It did, he thought, look like a grenade. Except for the seeds he saw poking out of the niches all over its surface. Seeds that were the same size and bright enamel red as Florence Varina's fingernails. The same shade of red too of the lipstick bleeding into the cracked skin around her mouth.

" 'It'll never take root. It'll never sprout. It'll never grow. It'll never be able to stand the cold.' If you had only heard the doubting Thomases, the worst one being my mother," she resumed her saga. " 'Oh ye of little faith' was all my daddy said to them, and after making sure to incubate those seeds for just the right amount of time, he went ahead and put them in the ground, including of course the one with Miss G.'s name on it . . ."

A theatrical pause. Then: "April ninth, eighteen eighty-nine. That's the day the lady in my front yard first made her appearance. One tiny little green sprout. And the first thing my daddy did was to record the fact."

She gathered up the worn Bible from the table, holding it up on the palms of her small hands as if it were the Host at communion. They would have a chance later on, she told her audience, to look at the entry, written in Gayton McCullum's hand.

"And years later when I went and told the Conservancy people about Miss G., they declared her a landmark. They came and put that plaque on her and started bringing nice folks like yourselves to see her and hear her story. Which pleases Miss Grandiflora no end. Because like all southern ladies, she never tires of attention!"

After the applause which went on for some time, the visitors continued to sit there like children at the end of story hour in a library, reluctant to leave, wanting more. An exception was an elderly man with a long-jawed face and the shock of silvery-white hair peculiar to them all.

(Hair, Sonny thought, like the wide billowy duvet of clouds he had seen from the plane window. He had been eager to inspect the face of the world below, but the clouds had hidden it from him.)

The man raised his hand to say he'd be interested to know how she had learned of the Conservancy.

A small silence during which Florence Varina stiffened imperceptibly, and then was quickly smiling, although somewhat too widely. "I'm afraid that story isn't part of the talk." Said with the too wide, mirthless smile.

She then invited them all to come and look at the entry in the family Bible on their way out.

Shortly thereafter, there was the sound of the van pulling away.

"Didja hear him? Didja hear him? He'd be interested to know how I learned of the Conservancy! What he meant, the old geezer, was how could someone like *you* living in a ghetto possibly have heard of *our* Conservancy. Don't think I didn't know what he was getting at!"

Sonny didn't understand her anger. There didn't seem to him to be anything mean in the man's question.

In the story that was not part of her talk, it was summer under the Franklin Avenue El at Albemarle Road, and the woman who had just hired her for a half-day's work kept stealing sidelong glances at her—at her clothes mainly—from the moment she stepped in the car. That day she was wearing an airy summer-print dress that had pretty cap sleeves and a stylish flounce at the hem. The white handbag on her lap matched her open-toe pumps, and as always, despite the heat, she was wearing stockings and a pair of short, open-work summer gloves.

There were glances too at her flawless pompadour. Pompadours and pageboys were just then coming into vogue.

She conducted her own sidelong appraisal. The woman wasn't much older than herself, although she had already acquired a kind of set, matronly look. The clothes she had on were of good quality but they might as well have been bargain basement the way she was wearing them. As for the way she'd fixed her hair!

Don't know the first thing about how to dress or carry herself. No flair. No style. No class. Pitiful. Florence Varina quickly lost all interest in the woman and turned to look out the window.

Her first task she learned upon reaching the large apartment on Ocean Parkway would be to walk the dog. It was a beribboned little Pekingese who ran joyfully to the door the moment the leash appeared. Along with the leash, there was also a large hair bow the same pink as the dog's ribbons and with a bobby pin attached. While still holding the leash, the woman had disappeared for a time into another room, only to return with the large pink bow. The bow was for her to wear, she said, smiling for the first time and pointing to the high front of the pompadour to indicate where it was to be pinned.

Cherisse. In the Armageddon of the moment, in the locked and silent war to annihilation that raged between herself and the coldly smiling woman, in the eternity before Florence Varina reached out and took the thing, she thought about her baby. About the extra dollars needed now that Mr. Jones was gone if Cherisse was to continue the singing, dance, and acting lessons. Her baby, who could be another Lena Horne.

Without a word, she accepted the pink thing, pinned it to the front of her pompadour, and took the leash from the woman's other hand.

Some weeks later, while cleaning someone else's house, she came across a discarded brochure in a wastepaper basket she was emptying. It read "Landmark Conservancy Tours, the Brooklyn Chapter," and was filled inside with photographs of statues, stone monuments, historic buildings, houses, and trees.

The next day Florence Varina appeared at the Conservancy office downtown Brooklyn armed with pictures of the full-grown magnolia grandiflora in her front yard. She also brought the family Bible with its date of birth entered in Gayton McCullum's hand and proceeded to tell the story of how it came to be.

It was every bit a landmark, she insisted, a local, even a national treasure. People from all over would be only too willing to pay to see it and to learn of its history. And there was the house as well, 258 Macon. It had been preserved exactly as it was when Gayton McCullum bought it. Indeed, the McCullum family had been the first Colored to own a house on Macon Street. That too a piece of history.

Florence Varina talking for dear life.

"I was the last and the first," she said, slowly putting away the mementos she had placed on the table with legs like a foal. "I was my daddy's last child, born in his old age, and I was the first child he had up north, in this very house. The last and the first. I come after Miss Grandiflora in the family Bible."

She gently placed the Bible back in the drawer.

Next came the cigar box. He reluctantly handed over the wax fruit she had given him to hold, that looked like a grenade. Her father, the man in the photograph, had searched the ground all dressed up in his old-timey coat until he spotted just the right fruit to take with him. The tree outside came from a seed the size and bright red of her fingernails.

"Varina . . ." She mused over the photograph for a time before putting it away too. "He went and put Varina in my name. As another reminder, I guess, along with Miss G., of the one place on God's earth where he'd once had his own land. He used to drill me in that story when I was a little girl."

She placed the picture, then the lace scarf like an altar cloth, into the drawer and closed it.

"So how did you like my tour guide talk? It was about you too, y'know."

"I liked the way you told it," he said.

Her arms went around him. A long, fragrant hug, which he returned.

After the embrace a final act: taking his face between her hands, she adjusted the corners of his eyes.

"Got the McCullum eyes!"

His also family and blood.

Hattie had never told him about them either.

11

"Wasn't that also when our homegrown
Romeo and Juliet first hooked up?"
"Yeah," Hattie said and abruptly fell silent.

Putnam Royal. Determined, apparently, not to let a day of
the two-week visit go by without seeing them, Edgar Payne
arranged to take Hattie and Sonny to Putnam Royal that
same Thursday. Hattie he said might like to have a look at
the place before the concert—which she did; she was eager
to see how it had been restored. So that at four o'clock that
afternoon, well after Sonny had returned from Florence
Varina's, he came for them.

Whatever annoyance Sonny might have felt with him
from yesterday quickly vanished. Because before starting
the car, the man made a point of explaining to him how to
operate the tape deck on the dashboard: the slot, the array
of buttons to be pushed and in what order, and the knob to
control the volume. He then handed him a tape.

He was to do it. Would he remember all the steps? There
were no such things as tape decks or CD players at home on
rue Sauffroy. A quick glance at Hattie for encouragement.

He was lucky and got it right the first time and a tune instantly filled the car.

He knew it. "Sonny-Rett Plays 'Sonny . . .'" A song he secretly believed had been especially written for him, his grandfather somehow knowing that he would come along one day. Hattie often played it on their old turntable record player.

"You did good." Edgar Payne.

He grinned and they were on their way.

The drive was a relatively short one. They were soon turning onto Putnam Avenue, a somewhat seedy, part residential, part commercial street, this particular block lying close to downtown. "We're working on Putnam Avenue too," Edgar Payne said and, amid the blight, pointed to a few renovated houses and storefronts, the handiwork of his Three R's Group. Then, toward the end of the block, he pulled over in front of a large, restored two-story building that had originally been designed with a faux medieval façade.

"Wait a minute, wait a minute, this can't be old bucket-o'-blood Putnam Royal!"

Hattie exclaiming. She was out of the car in seconds. Sonny quickly followed and stood gazing up beside her.

"It looks a little like one of your castles, doesn't it?" The man had come to stand at his other side.

"Kinda," he said.

He right away liked it, the building. And it did vaguely resemble a castle or a fortress he might have drawn, albeit a mini one. Stone. It was built of the same dark reddish-brown sandstone as the lookalike houses on Macon Street and elsewhere, although here the stone was rough-hewn and fitted together in large blocks. And there were a pair of turrets, real turrets, affixed high up on either side of the two-story walls. And with loopholes in the turrets from which to rain down hot oil on the enemy. And in between the turrets, joining them, ran an actual battlemented roof. There was even a squat tower; and, from atop the tower, a flag like a royal standard was snapping in the wind—the weather had turned blustery again. He made out a name and date on the flag. It was a flag announcing the concert for Sonny-Rett Payne next week Friday—his name and the date emblazoned on it.

"How'd you make this old barn look almost new?" An amazed Hattie to Edgar Payne. "It could pass for the Masonic lodge it once used to be. How'd you do it?"

"Shaking hands with the right folks," he said. "And smiling to beat the band."

"Touché," she laughed. "Boy, I could use a face-lift like this!"

"It seems you're not the only one who's impressed." He motioned over his shoulder.

When she turned, following his gesture, she saw parked across the street an oversize cream-colored '84 Eldorado that looked as if it had just rolled off the showroom floor. An old man wearing a Tyrolean hat could be seen behind the wheel, his face under the brim of the hat turned toward Putnam Royal.

"Didn't I tell you? Abe Kaiser. He shows up nearly every day. You can't tell him he doesn't own the place anymore."

Hattie's laugh had abruptly died, and she stood gazing in silence across at the car. She remained silent for some time, her face under the Sikh turban betraying only curiosity for a long minute. Until, a faint mutter: "Always with some lame excuse when you went to him for your money . . ."

Suddenly, scarcely checking the traffic, she stepped off

the curb and started across the street, not moving it seemed of her own volition.

"Where's Hattie going?" Panic. He had been so intent on studying the mini-castle he had forgotten them both.

"It's all right," the man stopped him. "She'll be right back."

On reaching the Cadillac, Hattie slowly circled around it to the rolled-up window on the driver's side. Bending down, still only curious, she inspected the car's sole occupant in detail: his hunched, aged body in the dapper suit he had on, a showy Mafia-boss handkerchief in the breast pocket—she remembered that flashy touch from thirty years ago; the knobby, liver-spotted hands on the steering wheel, and finally the face under the Alpine hat which was at odds with the rest of his outfit, a face skewed to one side by what must have been a stroke he had only barely survived.

She rapped politely on the window. Her voice too was polite. "Mr. Kaiser? Mr. Kaiser? It's Hattie Carmichael. Remember me? The Maconettes? I had a group called the Maconettes. You hired us for a while back in forty-seven. Remember?"

It seemed to take the old man a long time to realize that there was someone at the window blocking his view of Putnam Royal. Even when he finally registered the fact, his dimmed eyes were void of any recognition whatsoever; in fact, his gaze quickly bypassed Hattie's face to remain focused, although he could barely see it, on his former property.

"Can you hear me? The Maconettes!" The rapping on the window sharpened. "We were one of the girl groups you hired to sing on Sundays before the jazz show came on, remember? There were the Pearls, the Dynatones, and the Maconettes, my group. Don't tell me you don't remember!"

Voice rising, along with the sound of her knuckles on the glass. "You hired us but never got around to giving us a contract. Never got around to paying us half the time. Always coming up with some lame excuse. 'The place's not making a dime. The overhead's killing me. Not a dime. You should believe me.' Your favorite song and dance routine. Never mind every time we looked you were driving a hog bigger and better than the one you had the year before . . .

"You owe us!" Her gloved fist suddenly struck the glass. "You hear me? You owe us. All of us, and especially Sonny-Rett Payne who put the goddamn joint on the map. You owe him even more! I'm here to collect for him and everyone else. And this time you're not getting away with paying in kind like you used to with a lot of the musicians. Horse as legal tender! Bastard! I want cash. This time it's gotta be cash money!"

The fist like a battering ram, her voice a town crier's, announcing the wrongs of three decades ago to the knot of passersby who had gathered on the sidewalk to listen. A burst of wind along the street swelled the wide sleeves of her vast coat, turning them into a pair of apocalyptic wings as she suddenly shifted her attack to the car door and began trying to wrench it open.

"You owe Sonny-Rett! You owe us all! Cash money!"

Fear at last on the skewed face inside, the old man unable to ignore any longer the sight of the Furies that had descended on him. And in a single smooth noiseless surge of power the Eldorado was gone. No one there, not even Hattie with the door handle snatched from her furious grasp, so much as heard the huge engine turn over.

"And where'd you get the silly Heidi hat? Cheapskate! Bastard!"

Hattie shouting after him as a few of the onlookers applauded and the great car soundlessly disappeared around the corner.

She was breathing hard when she recrossed the street, still inflamed.

Hattie upset. Going over, he quietly slipped his hand in hers. And as usual, it worked. She suddenly threw back her head and whooped.

"I needed that! Oh, how I needed that! For years I used to dream of telling that man off but good!"

"Well, your dream came true," Edgar Payne said. "You put the fear of the Lord in old Abe. He might not show up here ever again."

"I feel so much better," she said. "Come on, let's see what you've done inside."

Inside, another whoop as Edgar Payne flooded the interior of Putnam Royal with lights. He even turned on all the spotlights above the newly built stage at the front of the huge room.

"I don't recognize the place," she said, amazed all over again as she looked around her.

"That's the point. You're not supposed to."

"All this space! It's got to be ten times larger than before."

"It is," he said and explained that they had torn down all the inner walls and partitions to create a space large and flexible enough to serve as a moderate-size concert hall with removable seats, a full-scale nightclub with tables and chairs, or a dance hall, as well as a center where all kinds of meetings, receptions, and neighborhood events could be held. There was a need for a place like that in their part of Brooklyn. It had taken some doing, but he had managed to persuade the people at the banks.

"As for upstairs"—he waved toward the second floor where the faint sound of hammering could be heard. "We've got plans for up there too."

"I need to sit down and take all this in."

Edgar Payne quickly left to get them chairs. He returned within minutes with three workers from upstairs carrying folding chairs and a table.

"The table is for my grandnephew here."

The man had thought of the table without his having to ask! The same as at the meeting the other night. When everyone there, including Hattie, had forgotten him, too busy talking—he alone had kept him in mind.

"He got a table for me, Hattie!" She hadn't thought to ask for it.

"I see," she said. "What do you say?"

"Thanks," he said and felt himself almost add the word *uncle*—Uncle Edgar—as he sat down and opened his drawing *bloc*.

"That must have been quite a day, that Sunday, when my brother played here for the first time."

They were seated not far from Sonny, toward the back of the great empty well of the room, the lighted stage way up front.

"It was," Hattie said. "It was a first for Sonny-Rett and a first for my girl group."

"You got your chance too."

"Yep. I'd been after Abe for weeks and he finally agreed to let us go on the early afternoon pop show that day. I was never so nervous in all my life, because what'd I know about managing a singing group. The whole group had the shakes. Except Cherisse. She was as cool as they come. She knew every eye would be on her no matter how good or bad they sounded."

A reflective pause, then: "So much happened on that one day . . ."

"Wasn't that also when our homegrown Romeo and Juliet first hooked up?"

"Yeah," Hattie said and abruptly fell silent.

And she remained silent, her gaze slipping its mooring in the present moment and slowly drifting away. Soon, she wasn't really conscious of Edgar Payne sitting beside her waiting for her to continue. And when he was called away upstairs some time later and excused himself, she neither heard him nor was aware of his leaving.

The doo-wops. The street corner, under the lighted street lamps, doo-wops with their tricky harmonizing were the first on that Sunday afternoon. Then came the R & B pretty-boy groups, all flashy choreography and waved, high-piled processed hair. Now, styling one after the other onto the stage, the solo crooners were having their public love affair with the microphone. Once they were done it would finally be their turn, the girl groups in their rented gowns and wigs, including the Maconettes for the first time, only here come a nervous Brenda Thomas her mouth all poked out talking 'bout she's not gonna go on. Her lead singer. Waiting till the last minute to show her skinny behind. Hattie could have slapped her. Instead, struggling to contain her own case of the nerves, she asked Brenda as calmly as she could what was wrong.

"You know what's wrong, Hattie. I'm not going up on no stage with Miss Siddity singing next to me throwing me off key!"

"Okay, Brenda, I'll move her."

Meaning Cherisse. Brenda complaining as usual about Cherisse who was positioned next to her in the lineup of four. Brenda had a whole catalog of complaints about Cherisse, although they essentially boiled down to three: she thought she was cute, she felt she was better than everyone on Macon Street because her house was the best on the block, and she couldn't sing.

"Chick can't sing, Hattie, you know that. She don't belong in no group!"

Hattie could have told Brenda Thomas that had it not been for Cherisse there would be no group. That the Maconettes, its existence, was solely about and for Cherisse. "Maybe if I could at least get into a girl group someday my mother would stop nagging me so much," her gift of a best friend had said their last year in high school, the two of them together on the bed in her room at Mis' Dawson's. "If I could, I'd rob a bank and go to her and say 'Here! Here's all the money you spent on all those lessons when I was small.' Then I'd just walk out that house and never look back."

Her best friend had brought up the idea of the girl group, and once Hattie graduated and was working full-time at Birdell's, she set about making it happen. She started with Brenda who lived on the top floor at 239, her family renters not owners. Girl had a pretty pretty voice. Then she had added two others from around the block: Evelyn Bates who had been in a local girl group before and knew the ropes and Vivian Adams who could read music. And Cherisse. The why and wherefore of the whole enterprise. Cherisse no matter all the complaints in the world.

Because what did a Brenda know? Had she been there the evening that her friend-to-be had turned from the dining room table and from her mother and father and searched the dusk-dark outside for her face, and with a depth of longing that matched her own? Had she been upstairs with them at Mis' Dawson's when they had become the kind of friends that no one, certainly not simpleminded Brenda Thomas, could possibly understand?

Now, she was standing there with her mouth all ugly, threatening to walk.

"I'll put her next to Evelyn at the other end, okay, Brenda?"

"Don't care where you put her so long's she's nowhere near me. Chick don't belong in the group nohow!"

The afternoon show was over, the crowd that went in for the doo-wop, boy and girl group, crooner music had departed and the jazz show, the late Sunday evening feature with its own sizable following, was under way.

Hattie was one of the faithful. She seldom missed a Sunday evening. And she usually came alone. Cherisse didn't care all that much for jazz. She sat now digging the sounds and privately savoring the Maconettes' debut. Thanks to Brenda—oh, the girl could sing!—and thanks also to Cherisse who had kept every eye in the room on her perfect self, they had easily won out over the competition. Abe Kaiser had agreed to hire them for a trial run.

She was by herself at the table, Brenda and the other two having left with their families who had come for the debut. Florence Varina had refused to attend. Putnam Royal? That dump where somebody was always getting cut at the rowdy dances held there on Saturday nights! The Maconettes? Some little nothing group from around the block with that "foster care" Hattie in charge! No, she wouldn't waste her

time. Nor should Cherisse. She'd never get near Broadway
or anywhere else bothering with some ghetto group
nobody'll ever hear of.

"That woman can make me feel so bad about myself I
sometimes wish I was someone else altogether!" Cherisse.

At the moment she was downstairs in the dressing room
changing into her street clothes. She'd be a year and a day,
Hattie knew. Her gift of a friend could primp some!

As for herself, in her role as impresario, she had gone all
out and bought herself a killer pants suit in black velvet for
the debut. The jacket was a cropped bolero-style affair that
opened down the front to show off the blouse she'd also
bought special for the occasion. A dazzling-white satin number with a décolletage that just wouldn't quit. And she didn't
stop there. To jazz up the black velvet pants, she'd hit on the
idea of placing three rhinestone stars down the length of the
fake fly. A Little Dipper of stars on her goodies. They
matched her rhinestone star earrings.

Her killer outfit and her killer hair. Because by then she
had started conking it. Every two weeks she not only braved
the men inside Duke's Barber Shop on Reid Avenue, she
endured, tight-lipped, the lye sting-and-burn of the Congolene that transformed her thick, unruly bush into a sleek
flapper "do" reminiscent of the twenties, complete with a spit
curl at either ear. Her hair slicked down flat to her head and
shiny as black patent leather. "Girl, all that lye is gonna eat
out your hair," people often warned her. She fanned them
down. Not her thick bush. At night, to keep her "do" in
place, she wore a stocking cap like the R & B boys with
their chemical waves, and in the mornings she no longer
had to hope, as she used to when younger, that ol' Mis' Dawson might think, just once, to comb and braid it for her.

Mis' Dawson. Hattie seldom saw her anymore. As soon as she started working full-time she moved out of the woman's house, although she remained on Macon Street, close to Cherisse, renting a furnished room and kitchenette in one of the growing number of converted houses on the block.

"Those old money-hungry W.I.s. Bringing down the place." Florence Varina.

It was nearing the end of the second set, the jazz show winding down when Hattie heard Abe Kaiser at the microphone call Everett Payne's name. Heard his name and, to her surprise, saw him slowly stand up in the bullpen up front. She hadn't seen him join the other local musicians, including Shades Bowen with his tenor sax, in what was called the bullpen, which was simply a dozen or so chairs grouped near the bandstand. The young locals gathered there each Sunday evening, hoping for a chance to perform. Because toward the end of the final set, the custom was to invite one or two of them to sit in with the band. They sometimes even got to choose the tune they wanted to play.

This Sunday, Everett Payne, not long out of the army, was the one being invited to sit in.

Breath held, Hattie watched him separate himself from the hopefuls and approach the stand, taking his time, moving with what almost seemed a deliberate pause between each step. The crowd waiting.

That was his way, Hattie knew. His body moving absent-mindedly through space, his head, his thoughts on something other than his surroundings, and his eyes (she had studied them well!) like a curtain he occasionally drew aside a fraction of an inch to peer out at the world. A world far less interesting than the music inside his head.

She had been among the first to see him when he was discharged. Still with his G.I. haircut, he had come by Birdell's to check out the latest sounds. What had come in recently? What did she think was good? Anything new by Bud? Miles? Bird? She was to bring him up to date, fill him in. He had some serious catching up to do.

The army—what had it been like, she asked him. No complaints, he said. He was lucky not to have been sent overseas, and luckier still that he got to play a lot of piano, and all kinds of music at that: the oompah-pah, military stuff in the band, light classics and pop tunes in the officers' club, jazz in the combo they had on the base. And the blues. The base was near Kansas City so that he got to hear and occasionally even to play some pure down-home Kansas City blues. That had helped his own playing a lot. The army? It had given him a chance to do some serious woodshedding.

Girlfriends? Had he fooled around any? Don't ask, Hattie, don't ask, she cautioned herself. You know you really don't want to hear. Besides, she could tell from the way—the new way—he carried himself, from the set of his shoulders even, that the old, around-the-block tease-name Goody-two-shoes no longer applied.

Where was he living? That she did ask. He had gone first, of course, to 301, but Ulene Payne, she had heard, had refused to let him in. She had asked if he was still playing the Sodom and Gomorrah music and when he said yes, she had walked back inside the house, leaving him in his uniform, the heavy duffel bag at his side, standing outside the locked basement gate.

East New York, he told her. He was staying with a musician buddy from the army who lived in East New York.

"All the way out there?"

"It's still Brooklyn," he laughed. "Besides, the cat's got a piano."

He hadn't even noticed the disappointment in her voice.

She watched now as he slowly mounted the bandstand and conferred with the bassist and drummer, those two were all he would need. Then, without announcing the name of the tune he intended playing, without in any way acknowledging the audience, he sat down at the piano and brought his hands—Ulene's large hands, the fingers long and splayed and slightly arched—down on the opening bars of "Sonny Boy Blue."

"Sonny Boy Blue!" That hokey-doke tune!

Around her, the purists looked askance at each other from behind their regulation shades and slouched deeper in their chairs in open disgust.

At first, hokey though it was, he played the song straight through as written, the rather long introduction, verse, and chorus. And he did so with great care, although at a slower tempo than was called for and with a formality that lent the Tin Pan Alley tune a depth and thoughtfulness no one else would have accorded it.

Quickly taking their cue from him, the bassist reached for his bow, the drummer for his brushes, the two of them also treating the original as if it were a serious piece of music.

Everett Payne took his time paying his respects to the tune as written, and once that was done, he hunched closer to the piano, angled his head sharply to the left, completely closed the curtain of his gaze, and with his hands commanding the length and breadth of the keyboard he unleashed a dazzling pyrotechnic of chords (you could almost see their colors), polyrhythms, seemingly unrelated harmonies, and ideas—fresh, brash, outrageous ideas. It was an outpouring of ideas and feelings informed by his own brand of lyricism and lit from time to time by flashes of the recognizable melody. He continued to acknowledge the little simpleminded tune, while at the same time furiously recasting and reinventing it in an image all his own.

A collective in-suck of breath throughout the club.

"Hattie, they're downstairs shooting up in the men's room with the door wide open. Am I glad my mother didn't come." Cherisse had returned from the dressing room to whisper in her ear. "And, wait, is that old Everett Payne from Three-oh-one up there playing? What's he doing to that song?"

Hattie silenced her with a look.

Where, she wondered, did he come by the dazzling array of ideas and wealth of feeling? What was the source? It had to do, she speculated, listening intently, with the way he held his head, angled to the left like that, tilted toward both heaven and earth. His right side, his right ear directed skyward, hearing up there, in the Upper Room among the stars Mahalia sang about, a new kind of music: splintered, atonal, profane, and possessing a wonderful dissonance that spoke to him, to his soul-case. For him, this was the true music of the spheres, of the maelstrom up there. When at the piano, he kept his right ear tuned to it at all times, letting it guide him, inspire him.

His other ear? It remained earthbound, trained on the bedrock that for him was Bach and the blues. All those years dutifully practicing Bach, Beethoven, Chopin, et al. on the old t'row-off player piano; and later, all those afternoons sneaking into Birdell's to listen to Muddy, Basie, Tatum, et al., never mind the beatings that followed. You heard them, both Bach and the hard, pure lyricism of the blues in that powerful, driving, disciplined left hand of his.

"Cat got him a mean left hand, man. Can't nobody touch it," they would say of him over the years.

He wasn't through with them yet. With the drummer and the bassist—the latter an older man with a humming jones—joyously following, he continued his soaring break-away course, charting unfamiliar terrain that was at the same time familiar—or so it seemed to Hattie, listening to the secret code beneath it all. For her, he was turning them all into twelve- and thirteen-year-olds from around the block again, strapped into the Cyclone and the Hurricane at Coney Island (five cents on the Franklin Avenue El had gotten them there), and they were repeatedly soaring skyward in the rattling steeplechase cars, close to the sun, high above the Atlantic nearby and with what they liked to think was a bird's-eye view of Prospect Park in the far distance and, beyond that, their world of Bed-Stuy, or Central Brooklyn; then seconds later, the cars plunging down again, taking them headlong toward what could only be an atomic ground zero, all of them screaming in terror while loving every second of it, their stomachs left somewhere high above them in the air.

Again and again he took them on a joyous, terrifying roller coaster of a ride it seemed to Hattie, and when he finally deposited them on terra firma after close to twenty minutes, everyone in Putnam Royal could only sit there as if they were in church and weren't supposed to clap. Overcome. Until finally Alvin Edwards lived on Decatur Street played trumpet in the school band got his arm blown off by the fucking Nazis leaped to his feet and renamed him.

Alvin brought everyone up with him. Including the purists who normally refused to applaud even genius. They too stood up in languid praise of him.

Putnam Royal treated him to a victory parade that Sunday. All the musicians, along with the hopefuls in the bullpen and a crowd of newfound fans, escorted him and Alvin Edwards to the bar that was over to one side of the club. Abe Kaiser, dapper sharkskin suit, Mafioso handkerchief flaring like an outsize boutonniere from his breast pocket, led the way, all smiles.

Hattie's table was close to the bar. Spotting her, Everett Carlyle Payne, who would be known from then on as Sonny-Rett Payne, immediately left the entourage and came over to where she was standing.

She placed her hands casually over the rhinestone stars on the black velvet pants.

"Hey, Hattie, I figured you'd be here. So what'd you think?"

As always asking her opinion as if it was the one he trusted most and the only one that mattered.

"You went on some," she said. "But you did everything with that tune you wanted to, and got all of it right. Every last note."

He considered this, standing before her with his shoulders still slightly hunched, the curtain of his gaze drawn aside only enough to let in the sight of her while the better part of him remained completely indifferent to the sudden hoopla being made over him.

Finally: "Yeah, I think I maybe came close . . ." Then: "See you around."

He started to turn away and Cherisse stood up. She had been sitting at the table all along, partly hidden behind Hattie, but now she rose and stepped forward to stand squarely in front of her friend. Fully in view. The milk-chocolate Shirley Temple girl grown into a beauty.

"Hi, Everett." A flutter finger wave. "It's Cherisse. You might not recognize me with this thing on my head."

She had changed out of the rented gown, but had left on the beehive wig.

"I know who you are, Cherisse."

The way he said it. As though he had been waiting all twenty-one years of his life to declare just how aware of her he had always been, confessing with the mere tone of his voice that out of everyone on their one block of Macon Street she alone had penetrated his cloistered boyhood, thoughts of her, daydreams of her, adolescent wet dreams and fantasies of her, her alone.

He stood there. The part of him that was simply a man helpless before her perfection.

"What'd you do to that song?"

From the way she asked, it was difficult to know how she meant the question, whether she approved or disapproved of what he had done or if she was simply trying to understand what had been so special about his performance that it had brought the whole of Putnam Royal to its feet, applause like a nonstop hosanna, like a thousand bouquets being tossed at him from every corner of the room. Nothing like it had happened when the Maconettes had performed, even with her up there laying claim to every eye in the place.

He gave her a vaguely questioning look, a shrug and, turning away, went to join those celebrating him at the bar.

Cherisse remained standing. She spoke, but to no one in particular. "I'm not moving till he comes back here and tells me what he did to that song."

Perfect arms folded under perfectly molded breasts, she stood waiting in the one spot.

Behind her, Hattie slowly sank down to wait also. She told

herself it might not be as bad as it felt at the moment; that in fact, it might be the way things were meant to be, the three of them like the connected sides of the triangles she used to draw in geometry in high school, with her as the base, joining them to herself.

It might be the way—the only way—to have them both.

"Hey, let's see what you've got there."

Edgar Payne had returned from upstairs and was leaning over Sonny at the table.

He was busy drawing the exterior of Putnam Royal, complete with its turrets and battlemented roof. Although he wasn't done, what he had captured so far was a close semblance of the building.

"Hattie, come see what our budding artist has done!"

The man was all enthusiasm, and when Hattie joined them, he said, addressing them both, "You know what I'm going to do with this? I'm going to have it framed when it's finished and put it up on the wall in my office, right next to a picture I have of the place before we restored it. This will be the 'After' picture of the Before-and-After of Putnam Royal.

"And you have to make sure and sign it when you're through!" This to Sonny alone. "An artist always signs his work. I want everyone who comes in the office to know that it's my grandnephew, the master builder, who did it!"

He was too overwhelmed to look at his uncle. His uncle Edgar. This time he heard himself, loud and clear and unmistakably in his head, calling him Uncle. He'd been advised to wait until it felt right. It did now beyond question. He could suddenly, without hesitating a second, say it to himself as well as out loud.

He nevertheless couldn't bring himself to look at his uncle right away, so he turned to Hattie.

He had expected to see her smiling proudly down at him. Instead, she wasn't looking at him at all, but quietly regarding his uncle, whose head was bent over the drawing. And there was an odd pinch of a frown, like an unformed question mark scarcely visible to the eye, marring the smooth skin of her forehead.

"You're going to give him a swelled head," she said.

His uncle laughed. "A little bit of a swelled head won't hurt him any." And turning to him: "I know it's not finished yet, but you must bring it with you tomorrow to show your cousins."

"I don't want him to have a swelled head," Hattie repeated, still with the little tight, barely visible frown.

As if avoiding it, his uncle kept his head bent over the drawing.

That evening she took a handful of her *médicaments*.

Hattie upset again.

12

*"Can you maybe come back again tomorrow
and the day after tomorrow and the day after
day after day after that forever?"*

The cousins his age he had never been told about. Whose picture was on his uncle's desk. Who lived with his uncle in a place called Long Island. He was at last going to get to meet them. The visit, though, would be for one day only, not the entire weekend as had been agreed. Because at the last minute and without an explanation, Hattie changed her mind.

On Friday morning, when his uncle dropped by on his way to the office to check on the time they would be leaving that afternoon, Hattie informed him that she really wasn't up to an entire weekend in the country, she wasn't feeling all that well, at her age she had her ailments, so that instead she and Sonny would come early on Sunday morning and spend the day. And they would be taking the train. It didn't make sense for him to drive all the way into Brooklyn for them. If he liked he could bring them back in the evening. But they were taking the train there.

Hattie saying all this in a voice that sounded perfectly

normal, ordinary, even solicitous: wanting to spare him the long drive to and from Brooklyn twice in the same day; yet it was a voice that left no room for appeal.

Sonny knew that particular Hattie voice only too well. As ordinary as it sounded, it was at the same time like the fortress walls in his drawings. There was no getting over it, under it, around it. A wall that no amount of pleading, tears, temper tantrums, sulks, or whining on his part could prevail against.

His uncle must have sensed this about it too. Because once she finished, he didn't ask why or demand the real reason or try to dissuade her. He simply said, "I see."

That was all he said and then turned to him. "Your cousins are going to be disappointed. They had planned all kinds of fun things for the three of you to do. But never mind, we'll make the most of our one day, okay?" he said and gave him the little uppercut caress on the chin.

It was the third one.

Right away he felt reassured.

His uncle Edgar.

As for Hattie, over the two days until Sunday it took a trip to Prospect Park and the zoo there, a ferry ride which he loved to the Statue of Liberty, the top of the Empire State Building, restaurants where he could eat whatever he liked, and on Saturday night a wonderful live show at a big theater called Radio City Music Hall to thaw his silence and win him back halfway.

On hand to meet them at the train station on Sunday were his uncle and the cousins, the three of them standing waiting in the bright sunlight of another spring-like day.

He pressed his drawing *bloc* tight against his side. Suppose they weren't friendly? And he allowed Hattie (whom he still hadn't entirely forgiven) to take his hand as they stepped from the train.

"I brought the gang along," his uncle said and led the cousins forward. Smiling, he greeted Hattie as if nothing at all had gone amiss with the weekend. She behaved likewise.

The girl cousin whose name was Kendall was a full head taller than him, Sonny noted, with legs longer than his, and she was dressed like a boy in dungarees, sneakers, and a sweatshirt that read "The P-e-a-b-o-d-y School." A large-faced Big People's watch sat on her wrist. She greeted him in French, saying formally as they shook hands that she was glad to make his acquaintance and that she hoped he was enjoying his stay in America.

"I thought I'd let her surprise you," his uncle said. "Kendall's just started taking French. Maybe you can give her some pointers later on."

Her American accent. That's the first thing he'd tell her about. He'd had to fight back a laugh the moment she opened her mouth. Also, she spoke as if reciting from a book. And there had been one or two grammatical mistakes as well.

The other cousin, the boy, came no higher than his chest and was dressed like his sister, only his sweatshirt read E-M-O-R-Y, and over a pair of eyes that immediately fastened themselves on his face, he was wearing a baseball cap with the large letter *E* on the front.

His name was Benjamin and he spoke in rapid-fire bursts.

"How come you're all dressed up?" (Hattie had insisted that he wear one of his new suits.) "And why've you got a book under your arm? We're gonna be playing! And why didn't you come on Friday when you were supposed to? We were disappointed."

"You'll have to excuse your cousin. He's six and still learning his manners," his uncle said, laughing, and led them to the car.

On the way there, he slipped the drawing *bloc* from under his arm. "I'll hold this for you until later," his uncle Edgar said.

"Do you really speak English as good as us?" Benjamin again, the moment the three of them were in the backseat of his uncle's car.

"Yeah," he said.

"All right! Okay!" and holding up the palm of his hand, the boy cousin proceeded to show him how to slap high fives.

He didn't know what it meant but he liked it.

His girl cousin also gave him the hand slap.

His cousins. He found himself thinking *his* instead of *the* cousins before the car was even under way.

He would turn his head into a vault like the one where they kept the money in a bank and there, for safekeeping, he would place every wonderful thing about that Sunday to tell to his best friend at school Jean-Jacques and to his *nounou* Madame Molineaux when he returned home. Beginning with his uncle's house. He'd tell them it was the kind of house you might see in the used *Marie Claire* magazines Hattie sometimes borrowed from St.-Joseph-des-Epinettes, that were filled with page after page of beautiful, glossy pictures of rich people's houses. It was that big, that beautiful, with a driveway that circled in front, a wide lawn that was already green, a large garden bordering the lawn, and tall

two-story columns on either side of a laird's massive front
door.

And there was a wood of tall tall trees surrounding the
magazine house—like a palisade of stakes he might have
drawn as added protection outside a fortress wall.

"Can't see what color your neighbors are, can you, what
with all these trees?" Hattie.

"Nope," his uncle said with a laugh that made light of her
barb. "And that's the way we like it. So do they, I'm sure."

Then there was his uncle's wife, his aunt Alva, the white-
looking lady with wavy hair and glasses in the picture on his
desk. She had the same name as her mother in the long-ago
snapshot. She emerged from the magazine house the
moment they drove up, smiling, her glasses filled with sunlight. *Gentille.* Nice. That was the only word for her, he'd tell
them. *Gentille* her voice as she greeted him. *Gentille* her
smell as she hugged him. *Gentille* the way she had dressed to
receive them, in a kind of colorful Senegalese boubou she
might have borrowed from Madame N'Dour, their downstairs neighbor at home. *Gentille* also the way she later
escorted him upstairs in the beautiful house when his uncle
declared that he needed some rough-and-tumble clothes to
play in. There, she outfitted him in a denim shirt, jeans, and
sneakers his girl cousin had outgrown.

"Now that's more like it!" his uncle hailed him when he
reappeared and then shooed the three of them outdoors.
This wasn't a house where children sat around watching TV,
he said.

His cousins had their own dog! Something else he would
report to Jean-Jacques. It was a medium-size dog with long,
floppy, silken ears and a pale gold, silken coat. A play dog that
didn't bite, his cousins quickly assured him as it came bound-

ing toward him, long ears flying, as they stepped out the back door. It spun like a top around him, sniffed mightily at him in his cousin's clothes, then jumped up to lick his hand. Its name? Cocker. "Because that's what she is," Benjamin said, "A cocker spaniel. I named her."

His friend would definitely want to hear about the dog. And also about the play yard his cousins had all to themselves, that was as big as, if not bigger than, their schoolyard. And where the yard at Ecole rue Legendre was totally bare, no play equipment except for the goalposts for "*le foot*" at either end, the only game played there; this one, his cousins', had every kind of play yard thing imaginable: a slide, a seesaw, a glider, two different size swings, a jungle gym, a chinning bar, a mounted basket and net for "*le basket*," and more.

His cousins' bicycles stood on their kickstands nearby. And within view of the play yard lay a fenced-in, covered-over swimming pool.

"*Tu mens, toi!*" Madame Molineaux would probably accuse him of lying when he told her about the pool. That would be too much for her to imagine.

To make up for the two days of the weekend he had missed, he sampled every play thing there to the point of exhaustion. Except the bicycles. There was no need for his cousins to know that he had never learned how to ride. His girl cousin, who told him she played "*le basket*" at her school, taught him the basics of the game, and after any number of attempts he made a few baskets. Benjamin, in an exaggerated batter's stance, demonstrated the right way to grip the baseball bat, how to swing with power, and they played that for a while. Afterward, using the basketball, he showed off some of the fancy footwork he employed in the one game played at his school.

"Retourne à la brousse!" *Philippe Télémaque, always a bad loser, had once screamed at him, red-faced, to go back to the bush, to the jungle, when using his fancy footwork he had slipped the ball past him as goalie and won the match for his team. Télémaque, furious, had even mimed a gorilla, swinging his arms, pounding his chest, and making an ugly animal face. Calling him a gorilla! He had gotten in a few good punches and kicks, aiming his foot at Télémaque's "zizi," before they were separated and punished. Both of them punished. For him, it had been only "des lignes," some lines: he had had to write thirty times that it was wrong to fight. Télémaque, on the other hand, had suffered "la colle," the glue: that is, he had had to stay after school, "glued" to the school, and a note sent home.*

He told Madame Molineaux, but not Hattie, about the fight, and swore her to secrecy. He didn't want Hattie charging up to the school, embarrassing him with her scrambled French.

After the play yard, he and his cousins had lunch in what looked like a small merry-go-round of a building on the lawn behind the house. A gazebo, he learned it was called, a place where you sat in the summer and enjoyed the garden, the sky, and the trees in the woods nearby.

His uncle waited on them, bringing them the food in a picnic hamper which he carried on the bald dome of his head to make them laugh. There were chicken salad sandwiches, milk, apples, and squares of a dark-chocolate, very sweet, chewy thing called brownies.

"Having a good time?"

Mouth full, he nodded.

"Getting along okay with these cousins of yours?"

Another, more vigorous, nod.

Then, as his uncle was leaving: "Where's Hattie?"

"Inside having lunch. She and your aunt Alva are busy catching up on old times."

He was really only double-checking. He had briefly caught sight of her looking out the window at them laughing at his uncle with the hamper on his head.

Above all, he would tell Jean-Jacques and Madame Molineaux about the surprise that awaited him later that day. After lunch, his girl cousin announced that they had something special to show him and, with the dog leading the way, he followed them into the woods that rose like the Berlin Wall between the house and its neighbors. A brief trek along a narrow path brought them to a large tree he couldn't name. A ladder stood propped against its trunk. He looked up, puzzled, and there to his amazement at the top of the ladder could be seen a house. A perfectly proportioned, perfectly built little house sat solidly anchored on a platform erected amid the thick limbs of the tree.

"She won't even let me come near the ladder when she and her friends are up there telling secrets."

Benjamin's wronged, unhappy whisper in his ear.

Awed, he scarcely heard him. His girl cousin, carrying the dog under one arm, was already climbing toward the house. Her brother followed, and cautiously Sonny mounted after him.

A floor, four walls, a roof, a door; there was even a window with a pane of glass, warm sunlight flooding in.

A play house in a tree! Wait'll he told them!

Once inside, his girl cousin declared that the place was chilly and they needed to light a fire. It could go right in the middle of the floor. She gave out assignments: her brother was to gather the kindling that was stored in one corner while he, Sonny, was to fetch two or three good-sized logs that would burn a long time. Directing him to another corner. As the oldest, she would be in charge of lighting the fire and keeping it going.

He stood nonplussed before her until he saw Benjamin, who had promptly scampered over to his designated corner, begin swooping up great armfuls of air—and understanding in a flash, he joyously went in search of the logs.

He returned staggering under a load of firewood.

When everything had been brought and placed where she said and they were seated in a circle of three, his girl cousin raised her forefinger for them to see, then struck it, a match, to the floor and set the kindling ablaze.

"Our mother's studying to be a lawyer," she said.

They had been warming their hands over the fire and she had been telling him about her school when she abruptly changed the subject.

"I know," he said. "Uncle Edgar told me."

"She's studying all the time!" Benjamin. An unhappy outburst.

"She has to, silly. It's hard becoming a lawyer. And she's studying to be a doctor of laws which is even longer and harder." This to Sonny. "That's why she can't visit as much as she'd like to. But she calls on Sunday mornings."

"And she sends us things." His boy cousin indicated his baseball cap and his sweatshirt with the letters across the front. "It spells Emory," he said. "That's the name of her school."

"It's a big university in Atlanta." His sister.

"All the way in Atlanta!"

"That's all the way down south," she explained. Then: "She might come spend part of the summer if she can."

"And the other part we have to go visit our father."

"Yes," Kendall said and lowered her head. She had her grandmother's wavy hair and slightly beaked nose, but she was as dark as Edgar Payne. "He lives all the way in California now—our father."

"So we have to take a plane and I don't like planes! They make my ears hurt."

His sister: "He's got another wife and they have a baby."

"And when we're there we see only her and the baby!"

"Our father's busy working. He's a lawyer too," she again explained. "Two weeks. We have to stay at least two weeks. That's what the court said."

"A whole two weeks!" An aggrieved cry. The next minute though he broke out in a grin. "Then we take the plane and come home to Grandpa's!"

The moment they sat down around the fire, the dog had come and stretched out beside Sonny, and he had taken one of its long ears and spread it out on his knee so that he could stroke it. He had once asked Hattie for a dog. At first she had said no. There was enough dog-do on the streets of Paris without them adding to it. She had quickly relented though. He could have one, she said, as soon as they moved back to Paree Cinq where it would be safe for him to walk it by himself.

He continued stroking the ear, his head lowered, as he felt his girl cousin's eyes on him. Stroking. Silk. This is how silk must feel.

"Have you been to see our great-grandmother?" she asked.

"Yes. She lets me play her piano."

"She never comes to visit us."

Benjamin: "And I don't like visiting her. Her house isn't nice and her hand the way it shakes scares me . . ."

"She can't help that," he said.

". . . and I can't understand that old West Indian way she talks. She acts kinda crazy too."

"She's not crazy!" As always defending Ulene. "Her mind just comes and goes sometimes, that's all."

"That's what Grandpa says too." His girl cousin.

The waiting silence again. Stroking. The feel of silk. Outside, a mild wind soughing in the bare branches that cradled the tree house, and at the window, the afternoon sun reaching a long arm across the floor to encircle them.

Until finally—Kendall speaking—he was being asked about his mother and father. Where were they?

He took so long answering, his boy cousin, whispering it, wanted to know if they were dead.

"No," he said and took a deep breath before raising his head to meet their gaze. "My father's away, busy selling things—I guess. And my mother . . ."

What to say about the runaway girl-mother who had fled after tearing up even her baby pictures? And why? That part was never included in what he overheard. He had learned everything about her except the "why" of her leaving.

"My mother's away too," he said. "Hattie, the lady you met, takes care of me."

His cousins nodded in perfect understanding.

Kendall then consulted her Big People's watch. It was time to leave. But first they had to make sure the fire was out, down to the smallest ember. She showed him how this was done, and along with the two of them, the dog barking at the thunder of their feet, he began stamping stamping stamping stamping . . .

He felt better.

Later, back at the magazine house, the three of them encamped on a rug in what his cousins said was the family room, he showed them his drawing *bloc*. He began with the drawing of Putnam Royal that his uncle planned to hang in his office once it was done; then he followed with page after page of his castles and fortresses, slowly turning the pages and explaining things as he went along.

"You mean you did all this yourself?" his boy cousin kept asking in awe.

He, in turn, kept nodding, until once as he brought his head up to answer him with yet another nod he saw Hattie again. This time she was standing in the doorway at the top of the stairs to the family room gazing quietly down at them on the rug. Or maybe he just thought he saw her. Because she was there and gone so quickly he wasn't sure. Besides, at the same moment, his girl cousin was claiming his attention.

"Who's this?" she wanted to know, pointing to the miniature knight in full armor and fully armed in the lower right-hand corner of each page.

"Me," he said.

Who was he guarding?

He told her. He told them both. He had never before told anyone, not Hattie or Madame Molineaux or Jean-Jacques, but he suddenly found himself telling his cousins that his namesake grandfather lived inside the castles and fortresses, placed there by him for safekeeping. And not only was he safe, he was healed as well, all the bloody head wounds he had suffered in the Métro completely healed, his head, his face restored to that of his billboard image above the entrance to the Club Belle Epoque.

"My grandfather's inside and I'm on guard" was all he actually said. "I move him to each new one I draw."

Again both his cousins nodded, understanding without his having to say another word.

When he reached the last finished drawing, he looked over to find that Benjamin had twisted his baseball cap around to the side of his head so that he could look at him more fully, without the visor getting in the way. Large eyes gazing at him as if he had suddenly grown as tall and important-looking as his uncle.

"You mean you really did all this yourself, no kidding."

It was no longer a question.

The awe.

The one-day visit over, night fallen, they stood in the driveway, light from the open front door reaching out to frame them. His aunt Alva presented him with his dress-up clothes in a neat package. He was to keep the play clothes he had on, she said, in case he came to visit again before he left. At any rate, she and his cousins would see him at the concert. Embracing him.

At the last minute his girl cousin ran and got her camera to take pictures of him with them all. Her own camera! He couldn't help it, but for a moment he was tempted to snatch it from her, along with the fat watch on her wrist, and run, run, run like the street thieves in their *quartier* taking off with someone's pocketbook.

Then Benjamin, unhappy at his leaving, was tugging at his sleeve for him to bend down. He had something to tell only him. His cap still on sideways and his hands cupped, he whispered long and ardently in his ear, his smell the meatballs and spaghetti the three of them had had as their own special dinner. His uncle had prepared it for them himself.

Once done whispering, his boy cousin then loudly announced, "It's a secret. You're not to tell anyone!"

He was about to promise he wouldn't when he heard the sudden, shameful in-suck of his breath, felt his shoulders heave, felt his eyes begin to fill, to burn, about to shame and disgrace him. Until Hattie, fathermothersisterbrother, saved him. The moment the tears caught him off guard, the wide sleeve of her tunic swept around him to cover him from the head down.

"He's sleepy." Her voice came to him muffled. "He's practically falling asleep on his feet."

Quickly she was bundling him into the back of the car. The two of them would ride in back he heard her tell his uncle so that he could stretch out and sleep.

But not even Hattie's arms around him on the long drive back to Brooklyn were enough to comfort him. So that when he was finally in bed, under the covers, the light out, he reached for himself, for his *zizi,* and the special comfort it alone provided.

13

"Got to have my beauty nap.
Without it, the day's too long."

Hattie stayed busy between the Sunday visit to Long Island and the concert that Friday. First, she began thinking in earnest about what she would say concerning Sonny-Rett's years in Europe, the memories, reminiscences, and "life stories" she would present as introductions to the musical numbers on the program. She actually started taking notes, working at the desk in Edgar Payne's living room. She reminded herself that the balance on her contract would not be paid until after the concert and she got down to work.

Secondly, she kept busy shopping, Sonny in tow. In addition to a laundry list of household items and small appliances which she purchased with the money she'd already received, she also bought presents for people back home. There were gifts for Madame Molineaux as well as for Madame N'Dour who had agreed to look after the old woman while they were away; presents, too, for Hattie's few die-hard expatriate friends who, like herself, also considered Paris home above and beyond any other place on earth. Paris, for better or for worse, till death do us part. The "Black 'Pats," she called them and secretly wondered if it hadn't been one of them who had gone behind her back and revealed her whereabouts to Edgar Payne. Or perhaps it had been one of those music scholars or jazz critics conducting research for an article, a study, or a book who from time to time managed to track her down to ask about Sonny-Rett.

"How'd you find me?" she had demanded and Edgar Payne had quickly ducked out the door, evading her question.

She also bought gifts for the *danseuses exotiques* at the Club Violette whose pale flesh she stuffed like so much used goods into the skimpy, sequined bump-and-grind costumes each night. They affectionately called her Mam'selle 'Attie and found her mangled, make-do French simply riotous. She'd been in the country longer than most of them had been alive and still couldn't speak the language. There was a gift, too, for the owner of the Violette, Marcel Ducongé. Another old friend. Before he had also fallen on hard times, he had owned a real club, a jazz club on rue des Lombards where Sonny-Rett had often played. After his death and with Cherisse sick on her hands and their money dwindling, she had gone to Ducongé, and he had rescued her with the job at the Violette. It was hers, the job, for as long as she needed it, he'd said.

He had also helped her find a cheaper place to live.

Her *médicaments?* Ducongé understood that need as well and kept her supplied.

A true friend. Not all the French were impossible.

There was even a gift for Monsieur Benhabib, the butcher. She missed him too. Although they'd been away for less than two weeks, she was beginning to miss haggling with him over his overpriced cheap cuts of meat.

In truth, she missed them all.

．　　　．　　　．

"Hattie, can I please go see my great-grandmothers? I can walk over by myself."

Nothing to do. He had finished the drawing of Putnam Royal, given it to his uncle when he dropped by the house earlier, and for the moment he had no interest in starting another castle. So nothing to do. And no one to play with.

He stood at the side of the desk where she was working. It was Wednesday morning and they would not be going shopping until that afternoon. He had dressed to her liking in one of the suits. He would have preferred the play clothes from Sunday, but he sensed it would not help his cause to appear before her in them.

As for Sunday, she had not asked him what had been whispered in his ear or why he had started to cry. "Everything's gonna be just fine again once we're back home" was all she said the following morning.

Hattie looked up from her notes, ready to say no. For days now she had been refusing to let him out of her sight.

He could walk there by himself he repeated, so she wouldn't have to leave her writing. After all, he was going to be nine next month and could easily cross the street on his own. Besides, didn't he cross avenue de Clichy every day by himself going to school? There were a hundred times more cars on Clichy than on Macon Street.

He spoke rapidly in French—which was easier—trying to head off her "no."

And he would make sure to call her soon as he arrived at each house and when he was leaving. That way, she could watch him from the window. And she could always call him if she thought he was staying too long and he'd come back right away.

"Okay."

To his surprise, Hattie said okay. To his further surprise, instead of the usual little perfunctory buss on either cheek, she drew him close and treated him to the kiss she normally reserved for when she was leaving for the Violette in the evenings. A long nuzzling goodnight kiss she bestowed on her favorite place on his neck.

Kissing him as if she would be gone for the night.

Magnolia Grandiflora. Origin: Varina, Georgia.
Planted April 9, 1889, by Mr. Gayton C. McCullum.

He studied the plaque, breaking the big words into syllables to make them easier to read, and then fixing each one in his mind. That done, he climbed the stoop of 258.

"Mis' McCullum been wondering when you was gon come see her again." Large Dora in her small apron and cap welcomed him at the double-leaf door with the rose window fanlight above it. "She's in her bedroom," she said. "She woke up feeling poorly this morning."

Poorly? He'd never heard the word before.

"Don't know what's wrong with her and she won't lemme call the doctor."

He followed Dora down the parlor floor hallway, past the living room on their right, to a door at the end of the hall. She eased it open, and peering around her wide hips, he caught sight of Florence Varina sitting half-slumped, her head drooping, at an overly large dressing table.

"Mis' McCullum . . ." Dora called softly. She had something, she said, was gonna make her feel better right away. Dora quickly drew him into the room, then stepped back, closed the door, and disappeared.

It took Florence Varina some time before she could raise her head up enough to see his reflection in the three-paneled mirror on the dressing table. It was a painful effort, yet the moment she saw him, she rallied somewhat and her arms opened.

He went and sat beside her on the cushioned bench that matched the dressing table and she enfolded him. With her arms around him, his boy cousin's whisper wasn't so loud still in his ear.

"You caught me without my face on." She was also making an effort to be playful. "You ought never to do that to a lady."

Her face was a whitish mask of night cream, so was her neck, the wrinkled skin there hanging in folds.

"Gobble, gobble, gobble." She caught him staring at it in the mirror. It was the first time he'd ever seen her without her pearl choker with the many strands. "There's nothing worse than an old turkey neck. It's a dead giveaway as to how old you really are. That's why I try to keep mine covered at all times."

She winked at him in the glass and slowly began removing the thick night cream. Even this was an effort.

There were at least three or four times as many creams, lotions, powders, and colognes on her dressing table as on Hattie's at home, he noted; and the bedroom reflected in the mirror was at least twice the size of their entire *deux pièces sans confort*. And nearly everything his eye alighted on was peach in color. Wallpaper, drapes, rugs, boudoir chairs, lampshades. Peach the lace scarf on the large console television. Could he ask to watch it? Peach the sheets and pillow slips on the queen-size canopy bed that hadn't been made up yet. Peach also the canopy.

And on the nightstand beside the bed, two photographs. One, his great-great-grandfather in his frock coat and spats. The other his *vedette* grandmother, looking like the movie star she perhaps could have been. Their two faces were the first to greet Florence Varina each morning and the last ones she closed her eyes on at night.

A telephone was there also and he asked permission to call and report to Hattie.

"Oh, just the sight of you makes me feel ever so much better," she declared when he took his place beside her again. "And as always you're dressed to kill . . ." She paused, a long pause, as a thought came to her. "What's the weather like out there?"

The peach-colored drapes were closed. It was night in the bedroom with all the lamps on.

It was nice again, he told her. He hadn't worn a coat.

At this, she weakly struck her hands together like a pair of small cymbals, her mind made up about something. Suddenly she was all purpose. He was to go and call Dora for her. She needed Dora's help. Then he was to go and wait in the living room. She had a surprise for him.

The surprise took some time to happen, and when it did, it came in two parts. First, it was Florence Varina making her appearance in the living room dressed for an Easter Sunday: in a powder blue spring suit with a frilly high-neck blouse, open-toe high-heeled shoes, handbag to match, *de rigueur* white gloves, and an Easter parade hat that was a cotton candy confection of white and powder blue tulle.

A boa of two minks, joined mouth to tail, circled her shoulders.

He couldn't take his eyes off the minks. The little flattened, rigor mortis heads, their glass amber gaze, the mouths clamped on each other's tails. Then there was the faint smell. The boa gave off an embalmed, mothball smell.

The second half of the surprise was that they were stepping out. She and her classy-looking great-grand gentleman friend were stepping out on the town, she declared.

"Didn't I promise you the two of us were gonna have some good times together before you went back to Paris, France?"

Behind her in the doorway of the living room, an unhappy, powerless Dora. She had been heard alternately fussing and pleading with Florence Varina in the bedroom. She hadn't ceased. "Please, Mis' McCullum, stop actin' the fool . . . You ain' able to be goin' no place as poorly as you got up feeling this mornin' . . . Oughta be in your bed seeing the doctor . . . Don't know what's gotten into you all of a sudden . . . Please. Anything happen to you peoples gon blame me . . . Ain' been out this house in years and now here you come getting all dressed up saying you steppin' out. And where you steppin' going anyway . . . ?"

"You'll see." Florence Varina, her arm linked with Sonny's, stepped around the sizable roadblock Dora presented in their path and led him out of the living room and the house.

Once outside, she stood for some time at the head of the stoop, unsteady on the high-heeled shoes and holding on to his arm tightly as she gazed around her from under the tulle hat. She might have been reacclimating herself to the elements of direct sunlight and cloud, air and sky, as well as to Macon Street which she had chosen to avoid in its near-ruin. She finally turned her attention to the stoop just below her, the dozen or more steep, dizzying stone steps, and she immediately called for Dora who was standing behind them, still fussing, at the double-leaf door.

"I think I need you and my great-grand gentleman friend to escort me down these steps," she said.

"You mean he'p you down!"

The two of them helped her down the stoop one baby step at a time; then, at her orders, they walked her over to the tree in the yard.

"Thought we'd pay a little visit to Miss Grandiflora this morning. I haven't been to see her for a while."

She sent Dora for a chair.

When the chair came, a high-back armchair from the formal basement dining room, and they gently lowered her into it, she put Sonny to perch on the armrest. She wanted him close.

To shade them, Dora had placed the chair under the magnolia's thick, luxuriant head of leaves, each leaf a dark lacquered green on top and brown-gold underneath. Because it branched fairly close to the ground, the tree effectively screened them from the street and the few cars and people passing by. It even seemed to mute the sound of the Three R's work crews busy rehabilitating the houses on the block.

Did his father, the former *vendeur* of picture postcards and miniature Tour Eiffels on the steps of Sacré-Coeur, maybe look like one of the men in the work crews? He had wondered this on the way over, seeing them high on the scaffolds, their hard hats a brighter, more vivid yellow than the sun.

When he was older he was going to climb the mountain of steps up to Sacré-Coeur and ask if anyone there remembered him.

One day he was even going to take the train to Marseille and Toulon, the last two places they had heard the girl-mother had run to, and there ask about her too. He might even be lucky and find her.

"My mother's away too."

His cousins had understood without his having to explain.

"... When I was a little girl, me and my daddy used to sit out here just like you and me are doing right now and listen to Miss Grandiflora growing," Florence Varina was saying. She'd been speaking for some time, her eyes shaded over by more than just the tree above her, and her frail arm around Sonny to secure him on his perch. "That was our game. My daddy and me both swore we could hear Miss G. pushing herself up out of the ground and reaching higher and higher for the sky. My mama said we were both crazy, but we didn't pay her no mind. And come May when Miss G. put out her big, old pretty flowers, the first one to show its pretty self was for me. My daddy would stand me in front of the dresser mirror and hold that big-old white blossom up to one side of my head so I could see it next to my face. When Lady Day and her gardenia came along she didn't have nothing on me . . ."

Sonny was about to say that Hattie often listened to someone she too called Lady Day—her sad-sounding records on their old turntable—when Dora posted behind them cried out, "Mis' McCullum, you need to come on back in this house and lemme call the doctor!"

"I don't know as I've sat out here since my daddy passed." Dora might not have spoken. "Sure never did with Mr. Jones, not even when we was courting. But then he wasn't nobody to be sitting out here with, a man without an ounce of romance in his soul. All he was good for was work.

"And did I ever with my baby . . . ?" Probing her memory. "No, I don't think I ever sat out here with her neither after she was just a little thing in her carriage. I was too busy, I guess, taking her to her singing lessons and such. Hoping maybe she'd be another Lena . . .

"That girl never knew how I shamed and humbled myself so she could have those lessons! A hair ribbon the same color as the dog's!" For a moment rage buffeted her like a sudden high wind.

"Been holding in too much too long!"

"Please, Mis' McCullum, come on back inside."

When she spoke again, she had calmed considerably. "But who knows, maybe she didn't want them—the lessons. Maybe my baby was just ordinary, average, and if I hadn't kept pushing her, things might've been different between us . . . Don't know. Maybe she wouldn't have turned against me so. Never a word from her till the day she died. Her own mother . . ."

She turned to him for comforting, and he hugged her. He was grateful that this time she didn't blame his grandfather and Hattie, and he hugged her, assailed by the embalmed smell of the minks, which overwhelmed the toilette smell he loved.

"Sometimes at night I ask my daddy if maybe I didn't do wrong pushing her like that. Don't know . . ."

He continued to hold her.

"We need for somebody to come along with a camera and take our picture sitting here all dressed up!"

She had rallied again.

"My cousin in Long Island has her own camera," he said. *For a single, uncontrollable moment he had wanted to*

*snatch it from her along with her Big People's watch and
run, run, run.*

"Oh, so you went visiting out on the island. I bet big-
shot Mr. Payne is out there living like white folks. Course
you wouldn't want to ask how he got the money."

He started to get down from the chair arm, and she
quickly held him back. "I know. I'm not to say anything
against those W.I.s got a claim on you too. Don't get all in a
huff.

"I suppose you're going to visit *her* after you leave here."
This after a long pause.

"Yes, I visit her the same as I do you." He was still
annoyed.

"She ever say anything about me?"

He could have said she called her an old-miss-young;
instead, he lied and said no, never anything about her.

"She better not!"

Another long, strange pause.

"She got anybody yet to come in and look after her?"

"No." He was puzzled by what almost sounded like concern in her voice.

"Somebody in her condition—old, sick, their head not
right—alone in that house. It's a disgrace. She needs to stop
being so stubborn and let somebody come take care of her.
Poor thing could die in there and not a soul would know . . .

"Dora!" A sudden plaintive, frightened cry.

"Yes, Mis' McCullum?"

"I think I'm ready for you and my great-grand gentleman friend to escort me back upstairs.

"And I think I could use a beauty nap right about now,"
she said after they practically carried her up the stoop and
back inside the house.

She took one every day she told him. "Got to have my beauty nap. Without it, the day's too long."

Back in the all-peach bedroom: "When you gonna come see me again?"

He had made his call to Hattie and was about to leave. "Tomorrow," he said. "I'll try and come tomorrow."

He was at the corner, waiting for the light to change to green before crossing, when he abruptly turned and started back toward 258. From his perch on the armrest of the chair, he had seen it lying on the ground under the tree, a slender branch no taller than himself that had somehow broken off, its green and gold leaves still fresh. He had seen it lying there and had thought of helping himself to it when he left, nobody would see him—only to have the thought slip his mind.

He quickly doubled back to retrieve it.

14

"I know the jig is up."

"Where you going with a tree limb to beat somebody?"

Ulene opened the basement gate wide, pleased to see him but nonetheless yelling.

Ulene. He suddenly heard himself calling her by her name in his head, the way his uncle did out loud. Ulene. The right and loving name for her.

"I ask where you going with that tree limb?"

He didn't answer, but taking the lead into the house, he marched ahead of her down the length of the basement to the kitchen that would have turned Hattie's stomach. There, he also kept her waiting for an answer while he reported to Hattie. He had to stand on his toes and stretch all the way up to reach the greasy, food-spattered wall phone, which had been placed high up to accommodate Ulene's height.

"It's a present," he said when he was done. It was the first thing that came to him.

"A present? For who? Not me! What kinda present you call this? Some old tree limb. Where you get it?"

"Across the street." Said matter-of-factly.

From under the battered dowager hat she wore all the

time, she peered with her clouded-over gaze at the magnolia's showy leaves, struggling in her dimmed, off-and-on mind to place them. When it came to her finally, her disbelief and outrage were so great she could hardly speak above a whisper.

"You mean you have the brass-face to bring something from that American woman yard inside my house?"

"It's a present."

"Get it from my eyesight!" A thunderclap.

He stood his ground in the middle of the kitchen, holding the branch upright at his side as if it were one of the lances or halberds he armed himself with in his drawing *bloc*.

His cousins were the only ones he had ever told who it was he was guarding, protecting, and they had understood without his having to explain.

"You ain' hear me? Get it from my eyesight this minute! Come marching in here with part of some old tree that woman's been fooling the public with for years, claiming it's a tree her father planted all the way back when God said 'Come, let us make trees,' and that her father—he must have been an obeah man—was the only body to get it to grow 'cause it wasn't suited to the weather up here. All of it nothing but some who-struck-john story. But I know she got people to believe her. Every week you see a van pulling up to the house. Foolish people paying good money to come see it and to hear the who-struck-john story. I tell yuh, I have to hand it to her. I thought I knew how to cut-and-contrive to keep going, but old-miss-young walks away with the prize . . ."

Ulene suddenly speaking with open admiration, even awe, until she caught herself and the old venom flooded her voice again and her mind reverted to the old wrongs.

"But she likes to scheme too much! Look how she put up that daughter of hers to turn my Everett's head. She was the one behind it. You can't tell me different. A girl spoiled rotten from small. That was somebody for him to call himself marrying? A girl with nothing on her mind but putting clothes on her back? But what, she get it from the mother. A woman that would go to clean the white people's toilets dress better than the Madams-self.

"Get it from my eyesight!"

He didn't budge.

"Oh, so you want licks!" She began casting around her, perhaps looking for the strap she had used on Everett Carlyle, her second-born, long ago—he who had been both her heart and the ruination of her heart.

"Get it from . . ."

"I need to put it in some water until I leave," he calmly said and after placing the branch across the seat of a chair— the only relatively clean, uncluttered surface in the kitchen— he started rummaging in the bottom cabinets for something large enough to hold it.

Struck dumb by his boldness, Ulene could only track his movements around the room, all of her at a confused standstill except for her eyes and the palsied hand at her side.

Amid the garbage, mildew, and scurrying roaches under the sink he found an old galvanized pail. In order to fill it, he first had to clear the sink of its mound of dirty dishes and encrusted pots. He took his time with this, piling them on the already crowded counter, Ulene looking on helplessly. Once he half-filled the pail with water, he added a pinch of sugar to it from a bowl on the table. That was something he'd learned from Hattie. She did the same with the discarded flowers they brought home from the Cimetière de Montmartre on their regular visits to his grandparents' graves. A pinch of sugar kept them alive longer she said.

He then placed the branch in its pail of sweetened water over by the window. The bright sunlight outside scarcely penetrated the years of city grime left untouched on the pane of glass.

This done, he led the way out of the kitchen.

"How you get so powerful all of a sudden?" Ulene cried behind him, finally finding her voice.

Upstairs, knowing what to expect once they reached the stairway to the upper floors, he stood aside while she yelled up into the nether darkness about the lights and the radios. A mind like the off-and-on switch on her piano. He was used to it by now. When it switched back to normal, he accompanied her over to the double doors to the living room, although this time he was the one who sent them vanishing into the walls.

Once inside the room, he reached the player piano before her, and quickly set about uncovering the keyboard, opening the panels to the paper roll, and then pressing the switch—things she normally would have done to start the music.

"Feels himself so powerful this morning."

She went and sat down.

"You ever hear of a big place in New York call Carnegie Hall?"

Eyes closed, left hand pinned down in her lap, she spoke from the clawed armchair that had been unloaded on her.

"No," he said and stopped playing. He was glad for the

interruption. The piano game wasn't all that much fun anymore. Not after Sunday.

"Mr. Cox—he was Everett music teacher from small—
Mr. Cox uses to say that with the right training we would
one day see Everett Carlyle in a swallowtail coat playing in
Carnegie Hall. That he had the gift. That's what Mr. Cox,
God rest him in his grave, uses to say all the time. When I
sit here and close my eyes I can see him clear as day in the
white people big Carnegie Hall playing their music better
than them."

"The concert this Friday is in a big place too," he said.
"Uncle Edgar took us to see it. You oughta come."

Her eyes flew open. "*Me!* I'm not setting foot!"

He quickly figured out she meant she wasn't coming.

"Had the brass-face to come round me playing the
Sodom and Gomorrah music! Not one foot!"

"Why not?" he persisted. "You don't have to like his
music but it's still him," he waved toward the top of the
piano and the picture there. "You oughta get all dressed up
and come."

"You . . . ! You . . . !" Ulene furious but at a loss for words
again. To escape him, she went and got out the dog-eared
photograph album. Dust rose as she dropped down angrily
on the t'row-off sofa, dust slowly filtered back down as she
opened the album to the snapshot of herself and her friend
Alva on Ellis Island, the fifty U.S. dollars that would prove
they didn't come to be paupers in their flapper handbags.

Ulene seeking solace in the cracked and faded image.

He waited and when he felt she had forgiven him suffi-
ciently, he went and sat next to her.

Silence for the longest time, the dust still settling
around them, until without looking at him or speaking, she

placed one half of the album on his lap, linking them, and he immediately said, "My aunt Alva is nice. I met her when I went to Long Island on Sunday."

"A white mice." Ulene sadly shook her head. "My friend from small went and bring a child into this world that looked everything like some little white mice and lose the good sleep-in job she had, her chances finish . . ."

"And I met my two cousins," he said, pursuing his own thoughts. "They say you never come to see them."

"I'm not setting foot!"

"Why not? It's nice where they live."

"They'll never get me to stay out there."

"You don't have to stay. You can just go for a day like me."

"Can you maybe come back again tomorrow and the day after tomorrow and the day after day after day after that forever?" His boy cousin had whispered in his ear at the end, and Hattie hearing the tearful in-suck of his breath had hidden him in the wide safe wing of her sleeve.

He felt the welling up again, the balloon of bad feelings in his chest beginning to inflate, and to stave off another shameful baby collapse he spoke faster. "I know what, if I get to visit them again before I leave I'll take you with me."

"Not one foot!"

He ignored this. "You can ride up front in the car and . . ."

She swung sharply to him, livid, almost knocking the album off their laps, and he shut up.

"But you know, you's as bad as that Edgar and the white mice. Those two wun lemme die in peace in my own house. Always persecuting my soul-case with one thing or another. I must come live with them. I must go see a doctor about this disgusting hand I got here that wun behave itself. I must let some stranger come look after me like I'm an invalid. One thing after another. The two of them trying to drag out my life. And for what? I know the jig is up. That the world don' have no uses anymore for someone like me."

Ulene speaking with a defiant coherence all of a sudden, her eroded mind whole and intact for the moment.

"I did my best," she continued, "and I did my worst in this life, never mind I thought I was doing right, and it's time now for me and all those like me-so to g'long. I know that. And I'm ready. God can take me whensoever He pleases . . .

"One thing"—she suddenly leaned close to him with her B.O. and the dank smell of her basement—"I'm grateful to Him for sparing me long enough to set eyes on the boychild. An easement. You don't know it, but you's an easement."

Easement? He didn't know the word, but from the way she said it, it sounded like a compliment. Her softened voice. Her grateful close-up gaze. Her arm near enough to encircle him. Not that she touched him. Not Ulene. She wasn't given to hugs.

Later, at the basement gate: "When you gon form yourself here again?"

"You mean?"

"And I can't understand that old West Indian way she talks." His boy cousin.

"I mean when you gon visit again! You don' understand the King's English?"

She was her old fretful Ulene self again.

"Tomorrow. I'll try and come tomorrow," he said.

He was halfway to his uncle's house when he remembered the magnolia branch in its pail at the kitchen window. He had forgotten about it. So had Ulene. He started to double back, then changed his mind. Let it stay where it was.

✦ ✦ ✦

True to his word, he went to see them both the following day. At 258 a worried Dora told him that Florence Varina was napping. She woke up feeling even more poorly this morning, Dora said, and had even had to cancel her tour guide talk, this being Thursday. Yet she was still refusing to allow her to call the doctor.

"Can't talk no kinda sense into Mis' McCullum."

Dora standing worried and powerless in the double-leaf doorway.

"I'll come back tomorrow if I can," he said.

On his way out the yard he stopped to check that he had correctly memorized the words on the plaque.

"*Eh bien,* one of my great-grandmothers in America has a famous tree in her yard. People pay to come see it."

Something else to tell Jean-Jacques and Madame Molineaux. Although his *nounou* would probably accuse him of lying again, unable to believe that any sane person would pay good money to see a tree.

Across the street at 301, Ulene, eyes and mind over-turned again, opened the dungeon gate only wide enough to fling the branch at his feet.

"Get it from my eyesight! Bringing some obeah tree limb from that woman's yard around me! I din' sleep the night with that thing inside my house! You's to get the rid of it before you set foot here again!"

The huge gate clanged shut and she disappeared inside.

He carried it upright in his hand—a piece of medieval weaponry—back across the street and up the block to his uncle's house, somehow feeling—a feeling that couldn't be translated into thoughts or words—that he had done his part, he had tried, really tried with them, the two great-grandmother women, his relatives, kin, family, and blood, and nothing more could be done.

"Whatcha got there?" Hattie looked up from her notes.

"A present to myself," he said. "I'm gonna put it in some water."

15

"Sonny-Rett Plays 'Sonny . . .' "
"Basically Bach, Basically Blue"
"The Crossing"
"Europhoria!"
"4th Century B.C. Stomp"
"In the Upper Room"
"P'tite JoJo"

"All ready for the big night?"

Edgar Payne in a tuxedo, a kente cloth cummerbund around his substantial middle and wearing a suitor's pleated shirt and bow tie, had arrived to drive them over to Putnam Royal.

As usual Hattie was still getting ready while Sonny, who had been dressed for some time, sat in the living room, waiting expectantly for what had become by now familiar footsteps on the stairs leading up to their floor.

"Yes, all ready," he said and promptly held up his left arm to show off the object on his wrist.

"Hey, got yourself a watch. And it's a beauty. When did you get it?"

"Yesterday. Hattie bought it for me."

After he returned from the aborted visits yesterday, the present to himself in hand, Hattie had suddenly decided to do some last-minute shopping, and once they were downtown Brooklyn she had led him into a store that sold watches and bought him one that looked exactly like a Big People's watch. It even had a tiny window that showed the day's date next to the numeral 3.

She had allowed him to pick it out.

"Here I am buying presents right and left for everybody except my one-and-only," she'd said.

He had hugged her right there in the store. How had she known? How'd she guess?

"Bet you'll be showing it to all the kids at school," his uncle was saying.

He nodded. First, though, he intended showing it to his girl cousin.

"I should get you something too for that drawing you did of Putnam Royal. A thank-you present. What would you like?"

"A camera."

He'd show that to her first, too.

"A camera it is. By the way, has Hattie said anything yet about when she'll be taking you away from us?"

His uncle's voice had suddenly changed.

"No." He didn't want to think about it.

"I know she said you two might stay on for a few days after the concert. If so, you could come out to the house again and have a little more time with your cousins. Would you like that?"

"Yes."

"Like it a whole lot?"

"Yes."

"Good. I'll speak to her about it," his uncle Edgar said.

In front of Hattie, in the hushed, dimmed well of Putnam Royal that had been transformed into an auditorium and concert hall, every seat was taken.

Above her, suspended like a banner from the catwalk of stage lights, was the large flag that had flown from the tower above the battlemented roof, that had Sonny-Rett Payne's name on it and the date of the concert, which was also the fifteenth anniversary of his death.

And behind where she stood at the lectern, which was positioned to the right of the stage near the wings, was the band, a dozen strong with the director, young Yusef Jordan in his kufi skullcap, both leading it and playing piano. Shades Bowen, his midnight glasses in place, sat up front, a patriarch on tenor sax amid the new generation of musicians around him.

To open the concert, they had played "Sonny-Rett Plays 'Sonny . . .' " and "Basically Bach, Basically Blue," the two songs he was most famous for, that had become signature pieces over the years. Once the applause died, Hattie had stepped to the lectern, the stage lights over the band had dimmed, and a single bright cone of light came to focus on her as she opened the folder containing her notes.

She was wearing what appeared to be her standard outfit, the loose-fitting, wide-sleeved tunic and long matching skirt that left her true size in doubt. Only this time, instead of cotton or wool, they were made of layers of sheer, airy georgette or silk. Black, of course, but with a dusting of beadwork at the neckline that flashed silver each time she moved.

A diva's gown.

To dress up the Sikh turban she had attached to the front a large, oval-shaped brooch that resembled a closed locket. Another dramatic touch. Whose face lay inside?

She first did a reprise of that Sunday in '47 when Everett Carlyle Payne was given a chance to sit in with the house band, and what happened within these very same walls when he finished putting a hurtin' on the hokey-doke tune. Silence like in church. Everybody blown away. Until one-armed Alvin Edwards leaped up and renamed him for life.

Word about him began to spread after that, she went on, speaking conversationally, Hattie treating the audience like an old friend she was reminiscing with, the two of them catching up on old times over a drink. " 'Man, there's this cat name a Sonny-Rett Payne can play him some piano. Cat sound like he been woodshedding all his life. Give him time and he might give even the Master a run for his money.' " Folks talking about him like that, she said, word getting around. So that along with the deal he had at Putnam Royal, the place packed on Sunday evenings, Shades Bowen among those blowing behind him in the band, he was also getting other gigs around their part of Brooklyn, from decent clubs like Brown's Cafe and Tony's to little hole-in-the-wall, bucket-o'-blood joints with a tired piano and scarcely room on the stand (when there was a stand) for the bassist and drummer in the trio he used on these occasions.

"But that didn't make him no never-mind!" Hattie employing the timeless, familiar vocabulary of around the block. Laughter rose like the gift of themselves the audience deposited at her feet. The gift of their total attention.

Sonny-Rett played, she told them, no matter where, when, or whatever the conditions, eager to show what he could do, loving to dazzle and confound.

ᔓ Wherever he played, she and Cherisse were there also—Hattie pursuing a counterpoint of other memories that were not for the public's ear as she spoke. She had disbanded the Maconettes by then. Once Cherisse declared herself: *"I'm not moving till he comes back here and tells me what he did to that song!"* she lost interest in the group and in singing altogether, and since the Maconettes had been created for her, she its raison d'être, Hattie saw no point to it anymore.

So that wherever Sonny-Rett Payne was being featured, the two of them were seated as close as possible to the bandstand. Indeed, Cherisse behaved at times as if she was actually on the stand, performing with him and the trio or the band. Because when a tune ended and the applause rose, she would often, without being aware of it, bow her head ever so slightly and smile, appropriating part or perhaps all of the applause for herself, in acknowledgment of her perfect limbs, perfect breasts, and the milk-chocolate perfection of her face. Her prized possessions. She had absolute confidence in their powers; yet, at the same time, there was also an almost abject need to be constantly assured of their worth, to be constantly admired for them.

The contradiction made it easy to forgive her vanity.

"Love? Cherisse? Are you kidding? Being admired is far more important to her than love any day! You know that as well as I do." Sonny-Rett to Hattie one night some years later in Copenhagen.

True. And neither one of them held it against her. Indeed, in some perverse and complicated way, it was what they both loved most about her.

And so Cherisse, in her need, appropriated the applause not intended for her, while Hattie with her at the table close to the bandstand simply waited for Sonny-Rett to come over and consult with her once the set ended. "What'd you think, Hattie?" How had the set gone? What about the new tune he'd played tonight? Was it maybe a little too way out? Had he gone on too long as usual . . . ?

As always she gave her opinion—the only one he trusted, she knew, the only one that mattered.

"You two! All you ever do is talk music!" Cherisse, having listened long enough, might say; then, with the smile there was no resisting, she'd slip a hand into each of theirs to draw their attention to her perfect self.

The Inseparable Three. The triangle Hattie had envisioned that Sunday with herself as the base, the foundation, had become a flesh-and-blood reality. And to think she had despaired when Cherisse stepped in front of her with the flutter finger wave? Now she would not have it otherwise.

She also began handling Sonny-Rett's affairs while he was still local, negotiating the terms of the many little gigs that came his way, seeing to it that he got to the right club on the right night at the right time, and looking after the money for him. That above all else. She quickly learned how to pitch a bitch when some club owner tried to pull an Abe Kaiser: *"The place it's not making a dime you should believe me!"* by paying him less than what had been agreed to. ∽

And word about him eventually spread to the City—Hattie still recounting the public saga—so that after a time his trio was being booked into clubs like Monroe's and Minton's and Connie's uptown and the Royal Roost and the Spotlight downtown. Sonny-Rett Payne playing the Spotlight on 52nd Street! By then he also had him a record contract, she said. "Sonny-Rett Plays 'Sonny . . .' " was the title tune of the first of three albums he made in '48. Three albums in a single year! And a number of the cuts were his own compositions. "Basically Bach, Basically Blue" being one of them.

The following year Europe came calling. An invitation to the International Jazz Festival in Paris in May, and after the festival the promise of bookings in cities across Europe. Le Jazz Hot was in vogue again and all of Europe was eager to hear him. It was what he'd been hoping for all along, she told them, a place, a country, a continent where he could breathe and create without a lot of hassle . . .

∽ And hassle didn't mean only Ulene leaving the basement gate locked in his face. Or the bitter memory of the strap. Or his guilt at having disappointed her. Hassle was also the Schrafft's restaurant midtown Manhattan where he and his accompanists, hungry after a long session in the recording studio, had been refused a meal. Midtown Manhattan now! Hassle was the same treatment and worse the times he went south on the road. The No Colored restaurants and hotels. The Jim Crow, KKKlan towns and cities. "Who needs this shit! I had enough of that in Kansas City when I was in the army. All you wanna do is play the music and you got to put up with shit!" ∽

Europe came calling, Hattie repeated, and Sonny-Rett Payne left the States never to return, taking his new wife with him.

∽ She alone stood up with them at City Hall. She alone saw them off at Idlewild, the two of them fleeing without a word to anyone. Their homegrown Romeo and Juliet. And when the news broke and the two warring houses on Macon Street bitterly accused each other, they also turned their wrath on her. She was behind it. She had aided and abetted. The foster care, City child without any background or family (Dawn, her mother with the pretty name, had died by then) had put them up to it. ∽

" 'The Crossing.' 'Europhoria!' Those were his first big hits in Europe. Listen and enjoy," Hattie said and stepped away from the lectern. A chair with a high carved back and the seat and armrests padded and cushioned in maroon velvet, a diva's chair, had been provided for her not far from the lectern, and she went and sat there, the layers of the airy gown slowly settling around her as light flooded the band and the opening chords of "The Crossing" filled Putnam Royal.

∽ Cherisse wrote at least twice a week: Paris. It was absolutely divine! A city made to order for her . . . She loved it. And it loved her. Everywhere she went she was treated like a *vedette*. (That's French for movie star.) The French definitely liked Colored . . . And talk about women who know how to dress! Just walking down the street here is like being on the runway at a fashion show. Speaking of which, she had found herself sitting not far from Josephine Baker at a recent fashion show. Oh-la-la! Imagine living in a city where you can find yourself in the same room as La Baker! And to have her actually nod and smile at you . . . ! As for Sonny-Rett he was playing, composing, and recording all over the place . . . He now had a manager, a booking agent, a record producer, *and* an entourage . . . People here can't get enough of him . . . ! He was doing so well they would soon be moving into one of the grand old *immeubles* (that's French for apartment house) in Paree Cinq, which is where the best people live. The building's old of course (everything here is old), but it's still fashionable and it has this cute elevator that looks exactly like a birdcage. She loved it. Loved everything!

But it's just not the same without you!

Each letter ended with that sentence underlined twice. She was to quit her job at Birdell's where she was now the manager, turn her back on Macon Street and everyone there as they had done, and come join them for good in the City of Light. The apartment in the grand old *immeuble* was more than big enough for three.

One of the letters bore a postscript: Hattie, been working on some new pieces I think you'd like. You ought to be here to give a listen. Besides, I need you to keep an eye on things for me, especially on the till.

Missing her.

It was then she made up her mind.

The elevator did indeed resemble a birdcage, all beautifully interlaced ironwork under a domed ceiling. But ancient. The night of her arrival, both Cherisse and Sonny-Rett had had to reassure her that it was safe before she would step inside the thing.

And the high-ceilinged apartment upstairs was indeed more than large enough for three. She was welcomed as they ushered her inside by the cool green breath of many trees through the casement windows that stood open to the spring night.

She stopped to breathe deep.

"Le Jardin des Plantes," Cherisse exclaimed. "We're right across the street from the famous Jardin des Plantes. Can you imagine! Trees, trees, wonderful trees, wait'll you see them in the morning, and not a single magnolia that I know of among them, thank God."

Apart from the requisite number of beds and a colossal new concert grand in the living room, there was not much else by way of furniture. Hattie was certain though, without even having to look, that the clothes closets in the master bedroom were already filled to overflow.

It was first things first with Cherisse.

No matter: Here again was her gift of a best friend looking happier, sounding happier than she ever had on Macon Street. And here, too, above all, was Sonny-Rett. At the airport, he had kept his arms around her even longer than had Cherisse.

"We should've made you come with us from the get-go," he'd said. "Don't know what I was thinking."

The triangle intact again.

Over champagne and some superlative weed that first night, she vowed that, like them, she would never so much as glance back across the Atlantic ever again in this life. ✑

"Europhoria!" ended and Hattie resumed her place at the lectern, the overhead spot igniting small silver fires in the beadwork on her gown. She expanded on the theme of the tune: the sheer euphoria of those early years. It had been nearly two decades of steady work, mainly in Paris, but in other cities across Europe as well—Stockholm, Copenhagen, West Berlin, Marseille . . . clubs large and small eager to book him. There were also the tours and concerts, as well as the jazz festivals at Montreux, Essen, and Antibes. Indeed, Antibes with its Roman ruins dating back to the fourth century B.C. was the inspiration for his "4th Century B.C. Stomp," the title tune of an album that sold big both in Europe and the States. His face was on the cover, and on the covers of an array of albums during that period. His head in its characteristic pose, tilted left, one ear trained on the bedrock, the other tuned in to the heavens.

Hattie cocked her head, demonstrating for the audience.

✑ "What'd you be hearing up there when you hold your head like that?" she once asked him.

"Up where?"

She pointed heavenward. " 'In the Upper Room.' "

She was referring to the Mahalia Jackson recording.

They used to listen to it together in Birdell's. As they did to Clara Ward, to the Mighty Clouds of Joy, and to the Five Blind Boys of Alabama, as well as to the ones from Mississippi. Gospel, too, had been his teacher.

He laughed. "Music," he said, "what else? And you can hear some way-out, wonderful shit up there, believe me." Then: "'In the Upper Room,' eh? I might have to steal that from Mahalia." ∽

"You can still see him with his head held at just that angle . . ." She was telling them about the billboard picture above the entrance to the Club Belle Epoque on rue Monge. If they ever visited Paris they should go see it, hanging there in permanent tribute to him.

"He was lucky," she added, "in that he worked pretty much all the time, which couldn't be said for some of the other black musicians over there. And I was lucky too, because whenever he played outside of Paris, I went along as his unofficial road manager. I was the one who saw to it that nobody—but *nobody*—messed with his money!"

Laughter and applause as she sat down again and the band swung into "4th Century B.C. Stomp." The tune featured a solo by Shades Bowen. *"Come the concert next week Friday, I'm gonna be up on that stage trying my best old as I am to blow a little tenor behind his memory,"* he had said to Sonny. The band would follow "B.C. Stomp" with "In the Upper Room" which Sonny-Rett did indeed steal from Mahalia and then, just before intermission, "P'tite JoJo," the lullaby he composed for his daughter at her birth.

∽ The road. Cherisse quickly lost interest in it, Hattie remembered. The other cities in Europe all looked, she said, as if they had been built in the Dark Ages. She didn't like them. Too much dark, gloomy medieval stone. They reminded her of those old brownstones on Macon Street she never wanted to see again. Paris, its boulevards and great public gardens, its *palais royaux,* cafés, and haute couture boutiques and fashion salons—that was her element. Paris. A city created with her in mind. No, she would stay home and work on her French. Hattie was welcome to the road.

"Why didn't you ever say anything, Hattie?" He lay propped beside her on the pillow, stroking the flawless mocha skin of her face, her shoulders, her bared breasts.

Four in the morning with the sky outside a numinous blue-white that was clearer and brighter than any dawn. The opening night of a weeklong engagement at the Golden Circle Club in Stockholm had just ended and back at the hotel they were being treated to a Scandinavian white night.

"Such as? What should I have said?"

"Something, anything, before Cherisse came on the scene."

From time to time he puzzled over their triangular life.

Hattie kissed him and reaching over to the nightstand helped herself to a few of what they both jokingly called his *médicaments.* He took them to mellow out after a performance.

"You know, you used to leave the records in a mess for me to put away when you sneaked into Birdell's."

"Changing the subject as usual," he said.

"And I didn't even have to ask if you had fooled

around any in the army. I could tell you had the minute you walked in the store that day."

"As always you're refusing to discuss it."

"What's there to discuss? I used to tell you how I felt every time I opened my mouth. Not that I could make myself heard over all the chords and notes flying around in your head. But how I felt was behind every word I said when we'd stand around Birdell's talking about a record. It wasn't only about the music. Not with me anyway."

"Oh, Hattie." He hid his shamed face in the curve of her neck and she immediately raised it up.

"No complaints," she said with a philosophical shrug. "Remember that's what you said about the army? Well, it's the same with me. I have no complaints anymore. Everything's fine. Everything's exactly the way it was meant to be. As for Cherisse, who's become more français than the Français, it's all in the family to her . . ."

("*Partager.* It's the verb 'to share,' " she had once whispered in Hattie's ear, seeing them off to a gig in Cannes—this was when they first started on the road together. Had whispered, then smiled wickedly and kissed her on either cheek.)

". . . It's only Monsieur Goody-two-shoes who feels he has to act the Puritan from time to time."

Laughing, she turned to stroke him now. "You know tonight in the club I wanted to take a compass—like the ones we had in geometry in high school, remember?—and come up onstage and measure the exact angle of your head while you were playing. I've been wanting to do that for years."

"I do not understand Hattie," he declared to the ceiling.

"Neither do I." She laughed again.

When he was ready, she slowly drew him into her wonderfully complicated, inexplicable self, proving to him, as she did each time they were together, that even an ordinary, unremarkable body such as hers possessed a kind of music, its own rhythms, harmonies, tonalities, crescendos—more than one, and that, at times, her special music had the power to leave him in tears afterward on her breast.

Pleasure that great.

It was also on the road, this time at the annual festival at Essen in the Ruhr Valley several years later, that she brought up the matter of a baby. It was time he and Cherisse had a baby. Before he could get a word out she clamped a hand over his mouth in the bed. Another hotel room, another bed. "I know, you don't understand Hattie. But please, for my sake. Everything will really be perfect then. Besides, it'll give Cherisse something to do other than spending your money in the stores."

JoJo Payne. Born January 20, 1960.

Cherisse insisted on naming her after the two Josephines, La Baker and Napoleon's empress. Both her first and middle names were to be Josephine. To simplify matters, they called her JoJo. For her part, Cherisse concentrated on finding clothes suitable for a little empress, while Hattie, who seldom went on the road after the birth, happily attended to the ordinary and necessary. She was the one who changed, fed, bathed, oiled, and powdered little JoJo, who gently and lovingly combed and braided her hair, the one who baby-talked and read and sang to her and walked the floor with her at night when she was colicky or teething. Hattie the one who would take her all dressed up in her empress finery down the birdcage elevator for walks in le Jardin des Plantes across the street.

For JoJo's first birthday she baked a cake and held the party at dinner that night, with JoJo in her high chair bedecked like her royal namesake by her mother.

The large gleaming table at which they sat, the table settings—the china, crystal, and silver—and the lighted chandelier above the table would have rivaled anything in Florence Varina's dining room. It was all Hattie's doing. From the very beginning, she had devoted herself when not on the road to furnishing and decorating the entire apartment. Cherisse had gladly left that to her.

She looked around her now at her handiwork, thinking of those evenings when she had stood, a prepubescent voyeur, gazing inside 258 Macon, hidden in the dusk-dark like a hunter in a blind. Some nights her angry longing was such she had wanted to put to rout the little milk-chocolate Shirley Temple girl—just drive her out with a whip or a club!—and take her place with a mother and father at the dining table in the pretty house.

All that pain behind her now.

She went and brought the lighted cake and after

they sang Happy Birthday, she helped JoJo blow out the candle.

Hattie, the materfamilias.

Cherisse, for her part, gave a little speech. In French of course, which is all she spoke now. And it was nearly flawless, her French. But then she had worked hard at it, taking daily lessons for years and constantly training her ear by listening to the talk around her in the cafés, salons, and restaurants she frequented with her friends, the wives and mistresses of other musicians and people in the business. (She deplored the fact that Hattie had no interest in learning how to speak properly.) Moreover, she had perfected the array of gestures and mannerisms: the play of the hands, the eyes, the set of the mouth, and the Gallic shrug—the hallmarks of someone born to the language. She would not be satisfied, she said, until her French was such she could pass for some well-educated Parisian-born second- or third-generation Francophone African, or an Antillaise from Martinique or Guadeloupe.

"I sometimes wish I was someone else altogether!" she had cried years ago, despairing of herself in the face of Florence Varina's impossible ambitions for her.

Her glass of champagne raised, she assured JoJo in her near-flawless French that she was going to outstrip her two namesakes, in that she would be more talented and famous than La Baker and a greater beauty than Napoleon's Josephine. She was to take her mother's word for it. All the signs were there.

JoJo with her baby fat and as yet scarcely defined little features. They all laughed and Sonny-Rett, with them at the table, their threesome ménage intact, also raised his glass in a birthday toast to his daughter. With JoJo, the drawn curtain that guarded his gaze at all times, that he drew aside no more than a fraction of an inch to peer out occasionally at the world that was apart from the world of music inside his head, always stood wide open in her presence. The curtain opened all the way to take in the miracle of her.

Hadn't Hattie told him in the hotel in Essen in the Ruhr Valley that a baby would make everything perfect?

As for JoJo, all along she had found the party hat on her head something of a nuisance, especially the chafing rubber band under her chin that held it on. So that now that the presents had been opened, the cake sampled, the singing done, and yet more pictures taken of her to add to the already burgeoning photograph album devoted solely to her image; now, moreover, that there was no longer the bright dancing light of the candle to distract her, she reached up and tore the thing off her head.

She had had enough birthday and, bypassing her mother and her worshipful father, she held out her arms to Hattie. Hattie was to take her.

"P'tite JoJo." Her father composed a lullaby like none other in her name.

It too became one of his signature tunes. ∽

"That's my mother's song," Sonny whispered to his cousins seated with him in the front row as the strains of "P'tite JoJo" rose to fill Putnam Royal. "It was written just for her."

When he was small Madame Molineaux, at Hattie's instructions, would play it each night to put him to sleep.

When he was older he would go looking for her in Marseille and Toulon. JoJo, the runaway.

16

"Continental Free-fall"
"Sodom and Gomorrah Days and Nights"
"Sonny-Rett Plays 'Sonny . . .'" Reprise

Intermission over, Hattie took her place at the lectern again. In contrast to her conversational, "around-the-block" manner that had quickly won over the audience, she began speaking this time in a surprisingly flat, factual voice about the jazz scene in Europe, how it started to change around the mid-sixties, especially in France. There were suddenly all these new cabaret laws and rules on the books, she told them. She even cited some of them: There were to be no more all-black bands, for one. French musicians, nationals, had to be included; in fact, they were to be given preference when a club was hiring. The playing of non-French music on the radio was to be strictly limited. Another law. Non-French music meaning jazz, not Beethoven or Bach, she pointed out. For years the state radio in Paris had regularly played live jazz, commissioning prominent musicians like Sonny-Rett—who were considered almost French by then—to compose and arrange the music for the various studio bands. That too soon came to an end.

And it wasn't only France. The whole of Europe, she said, had changed as far as jazz was concerned. The novelty had worn thin. Their own were being hired. Moreover, the art of those like Sonny-Rett was being supplanted more and more by "a whole lotta noise that the white boys playing it had the nerve to call Rock and Roll and even Rhythm and Blues. Stealing our stuff. Don't think 'cause I was over there in Europe I didn't know what was happening. Like it says in that poem by Langston Hughes—Mr. Hughes—'You done taken my blues and gone.' And look what you went and did to it I would've added: Noise."

Applause at her sudden outburst.

"Preach!" a voice exhorted her above the clapping.

Any number of black musicians got the message and left for home, Hattie went on to say after composing herself, continuing the history lesson Shades Bowen had urged her to give "the young folks" at the meeting last week in Edgar Payne's office. It was back to the States for better or for worse, she informed them. For Sonny-Rett the choice remained Europe, meaning Paris. And that proved to be for the worse. Less and less of the kind of work he was used to came his way: the regular bookings at the big, well-known clubs, the record dates, the concerts, the yearly festivals. Less of all that, including even the standard engagement at the Belle Epoque where his image hung out front . . .

She paused, raised her aging face into the cone of light, searching for a way to describe those down-spiraling five or six years before his death (years that seemed like decades!), what they did to him, Hattie waiting for the words to come, the beadwork at her neck and the closed locket of a brooch on her turban glinting in the darkened well of the hall.

The audience respectfully waited with her.

Finally: "You could say that his life then became a long free-fall down the steps of the Paris subway years before that awful thing actually happened. He was living the way he would die—falling. Seems like he even knew it—y'know, a death foretold—because it was during those years that he composed 'Continental Free-fall' as well as 'Sodom and Gomorrah Days and Nights.' You can hear the long free-fall in both those tunes. Listen."

For the last time she closed the folder with her notes (she had scarcely consulted them all evening) and returned to her seat.

⌒ 4 April 1969. The police, *les flics,* cracking down on the undocumented, the illegals, stopped him that Friday night in the Châtelet station. He was on his way from a little catch-as-catch-can gig, substituting for the regular pianist in a small piano bar amid the *boîtes* and *caves* of Les Halles. The great Sonny-Rett Payne playing piano bar! According to the police report, when asked for his *Carte de résident* (which, as always, was in his wallet), he told them they could find it hanging above the entrance to a certain nightclub on rue Monge. High. Stoned. He must have been stoned out of his mind to have said that, Hattie knew, too many of the *médicaments* combined with the drinks of whatever kind that had also become a staple with him. A combination that instead of salving his despair only deepened it. After telling *les flics* where to find his residency card, he had then walked away, the report claimed, and when an attempt was made to arrest him, he had broken free of the two policemen and, sprinting ahead of them, had either fallen or jumped down the long flight of concrete stairs, repeatedly striking his head on the way down.

Only *les flics* had been there.

Having long accepted her lesser role, Cherisse deferred to Hattie in making the funeral arrangements.

"I'll always remember him huddled with you at a table in some club talking music," she said, the two of them holding their own private wake after the official one was over and nine-year-old JoJo, stricken silent by her father's death, was finally asleep. They were still living in the old *immeuble* in Paree Cinq. By dint of Hattie carefully managing the dwindling "till" and Sonny-Rett's little pickup gigs here and there, they had managed to hold on to the apartment.

"With him it was always Hattie first." Cherisse trying to comfort a Hattie who, crumpled beside her on the sofa, was, for the time being, beyond comforting. "First in everything. Me, I never minded so long as the three of us were together. You know that. Besides, didn't ol' Everett Payne rescue me from that woman at Two fifty-eight Macon. Don't think I didn't love him for that."

She spoke in English. It was one of those rare occasions when she reverted to English.

Cherisse even left it to Hattie to write to Ulene Payne with the news.

Four years later, there would be another letter like it for her to write when Cherisse herself died. In it, Hattie didn't tell Florence Varina that it had been a needless death, that the doctors had said the small tumor could be easily removed and the breast as easily reconstructed afterward.

"*I am not having anybody cut on me!*" Speaking English again as she stood with Hattie outside the doctor's office, frightened but nonetheless willful, arms folded under the once-perfect breasts and sounding pure Macon Street, pure Brooklyn.

"No way! Besides, I've never felt better."

No matter how hard Hattie tried, there was no dissuading her, no reasoning with her. Following her own mind, Cherisse took the better part of the life insurance money Sonny-Rett had left them—money they were using to live on—and entered an alternative clinic in Germany.

Cherisse left for Germany, flying there instead of taking the train which would have been cheaper, and Hattie, after she and JoJo saw her off at Orly, immediately went to Marcel Ducongé, her old friend who owned the Violette, to ask his help: a job, a cheap place to live, no matter what *arrondissement,* what *quartier.*

Hattie desperate. The clinic Cherisse had chosen was one of the most expensive in Germany.

The day before they moved to rue Sauffroy, she and JoJo went for a late-afternoon walk, their last, in le Jardin des Plantes. It was the final week in April and the kind of weather celebrated in the famous song about the city during that month. The spring rains were just about over, the sky a clear washed cerulean, le Jardin des Plantes in glorious bloom and the chestnut trees lining the fashionable boulevards decked out in blossoms the shape of miniature Christmas trees.

JoJo. She moved like a sleepwalker alongside Hattie, dark head bowed, shrunken into silence again by this latest blow. It was as if she had taken her numbed self and gone into hiding, leaving behind only the shell of her body in the clothes she'd worn to school—dark blue plaid skirt, white Peter Pan blouse, and a cardigan a lighter blue than the skirt.

This was also her last day at her lycée.

"Can you remember when you tried climbing that tree over there? You must have been six or seven."

Hattie trying to rouse her. She was pointing to a low-branching deodar cedar off to their left, an old, majestic mother tree with wide, embracing arms.

Silence. The head with the braided ponytail and bangs Hattie had fixed that morning remained bowed. The feet in the schoolgirl oxfords and kneesocks moved dully ahead.

"You suddenly dropped my hand and went tearing off when you saw some boys climbing it. You wanted to also. That huge thing with all those needles. And never mind you were all dressed up. It was a Sunday and you were wearing that yellow dress with the peplum you liked so much. I don't suppose you remember that dress . . . ?"

"I don't wanna remember anything!"

An almost angry mutter from the hiding place, in the English she had learned from Hattie. (She spoke her mother's impeccable French as well.) JoJo sounded as if all the things that had once defined her—her neat clothes, her school where, until her father's death, she had nearly always been *première de la classe;* her friends at school, her own large, sunny bedroom in the building with the birdcage elevator where she had lived since birth, also the father and mother who had made possible her birth and even *Hattie*—that all these things had suddenly proved unreliable, untrustworthy, and therefore somehow worthless. And that the same applied to herself. Indeed, it was the way she started to behave almost overnight once they moved, becoming a JoJo who, in spite of Hattie's efforts, no longer cared about school or the way she dressed or spoke or the kinds of friends she made at school or in the *quartier* . . .

"I know you're worried but, you watch, your mama's gonna be all right."

Hattie had had her arm around her all along, and now she drew her closer.

JoJo stopped, slipped out from under the arm around her, and, at last, raised her head. The look she gave Hattie. It was the same one she had bent on her mother at the airport, when Cherisse had cheerfully promised her she would be back in no time a hundred percent cured. JoJo had quietly regarded her mother as though the tables were turned, the roles reversed, and she, the child, was the adult who knew better.

She looked at Hattie the same way that last day in the garden of plants.

"Everybody here swears there's not a thing wrong with me I look so good!" All of Cherisse's letters read the same. But the herbs, supplements, colonics, apricot pits, and other esoteric therapies didn't help, her condition steadily worsened, and when she could no longer pay, Hattie went and brought her back to the *deux pièces sans confort* on the top floor of 130, rue Sauffroy.

Up to the end she nursed her all day, and sometimes, on the nights when she didn't work, Hattie held her—a mere wraith—in the bed and ever so gently loved her as when they were girls practicing their kissing and touching upstairs at Mis' Dawson's, reassuring her gift of a best friend that she would always possess the power to draw every eye in a room to her perfect self.

When did she finally become conscious of the sound that was scarcely a sound: the warped door to JoJo's tiny bedroom that never closed flush being eased open an inch wider? When was she finally aware of what could only be the white of an eye, the sole thing visible in the darkness, looking on? How many nights had JoJo, fourteen by then, stood silently watching before she fled, leaving every picture ever taken of her shredded beyond recognition on the floor in her room?

No more than a month later, Hattie lovingly placed Cherisse next to Sonny-Rett in Cimetière de Montmartre, and after writing to Florence Varina, she locked herself in the apartment. Outside the door Madame Molineaux and Madame N'Dour pleaded in vain to be allowed in. But she again refused to be comforted. Off and on, day and night, she sat on the floor in the tiny bedroom, her bared head revealing the damage the Congolene long ago had done to her thick bush of hair, her body bowed under the stone weight of her grief, surrounded by the carnage of photographs JoJo had left behind.

Hattie sitting shiva for them both.

〃   〃   〃

A year later, 1975, JoJo briefly returned, although Hattie didn't get to see her. One morning she heard Madame N'Dour's frantic voice downstairs calling JoJo's name as well as her own. And when she ran down to the fourth floor, her heart almost failing her, she found her neighbor standing shaken and confused in the doorway of her apartment, holding the baby JoJo had thrust in her arms with instructions to give it to the *gouine!* upstairs before she fled again.

The father? An eighteen-year-old former *vendeur* on the steps of Sacré-Coeur, *un sans papiers* who weeks earlier had been caught and deported to his native Cameroon. This according to Madame N'Dour's teenage daughter who had heard the talk going around. Later, the girl also learned that right after handing over the baby JoJo had left for either Marseille or Toulon, but more likely Toulon where there was a naval base.

P'tite JoJo, who was really Hattie's child. Wasn't she, after all, the one who had given birth to the idea of her? Hadn't she, to all effects, raised her, a mother in act and deed and love, if not in name? Only to have JoJo refuse to so much as give her a chance to explain . . .

But then Hattie considered her good fortune in the gift Madame N'Dour turned over to her. It had slept through all the commotion. Back upstairs, she again locked the door to everyone and, alone in the *deux pièces,* she first slowly unfolded the none-too-clean receiving blanket. A note pinned inside gave the birth date, 14 Mai, but no name. Then, like a curator appraising a masterpiece new to a collection, Hattie minutely examined the rare find from head to toe, lingering on the small still life of a face that didn't as yet have its full, rich color. To her eye, it reflected them all: Sonny-Rett, Cherisse, JoJo. A triple exposure, that little face. The outward and visible sign of their continuing presence. It contained all three of her loves; moreover, it restored them to her intact, along with the life they'd had together.

"There're all kinds of family and blood's got nothing to do with it!"

She had had to straighten out Edgar Payne about that.

The gift awoke, and the tiny head she could easily cup in her hand immediately turned toward the warmth and solidity of her body, and the mouth that was unmistakably his grandfather's began rooting for her breast.

He would be hers for the rest of her lifetime. She would do whatever it took to see to that.

She named him Sonny Carmichael Payne and found herself *un avocat louche*—the kind who didn't ask questions—to provide her with the necessary papers. She then wrote once again and for the last time to both Ulene Payne and Florence Varina, informing them of his birth, the circumstances surrounding it, and the fact of her "legal" custody.

Neither of the letters bore a return address.

Nor had the other two she'd written before. ∽

"Sonny-Rett Plays 'Sonny . . .' " Reprise.

The reprise of the signature tune that ended the concert was a different arrangement altogether from the version at the beginning. And it opened with another solo by Shades Bowen. This time, with the spotlight on him alone and his sax canted toward the banner above the stage, he transformed the old Tin Pan Alley song into a tender, complex, and eloquent New Orleans processional dirge out to the burial ground. His tenor, with its natural sweetness, not only bringing home Sonny-Rett Payne, born Everett Carlyle, Ulene's boychild, but also bidding him a respectful and loving farewell, putting him to rest properly on native ground.

"Take your time! Take your time!" A call from the audience.

Shades took his time and put him to rest properly.

That done, the lights went up, the brass section of the band rose to its feet, and with Shades leading the way, the procession back from the grave was, in the tradition, a sudden uptempo, swinging, joyous celebration of the man and his art.

At the end, the applause became a long loud coda that went on endlessly. Beaming, Yusef Jordan came over and escorted Hattie center stage. There, they were joined by Shades Bowen as well as Edgar Payne who had also brought Sonny up to be introduced to the crowd.

The namesake grandson.

Hattie holding on to Sonny's hand gave a diva's sweeping bow and the applause soared higher. She immediately deflected it from herself and, with her other hand raised high, hailed the banner that bore the honoree's name.

The entire auditorium rose to its feet.

"We know where he really is, don't we?" his boy cousin had whispered to Sonny just before his uncle came to take him onstage.

He meant safely inside the drawing *bloc*.

17

"Money! Money'll do it every time!"

As he curled into sleep, still warm from his uncle's arms that had once again half-carried him up the stairs (although this time he had pretended to be sleepier than he actually was so's to be carried), he heard Hattie in the living room saying—and she was speaking pleasantly enough—that she really didn't remember promising . . . something or the other.

He didn't make out what the "something" was. Sleep overtaking him.

"But if I did promise that, it's out of the question now. We can't possibly stay any longer. I've got a job to get back to and Sonny's got school. I'm sure you can understand that. No, we're leaving this Sunday. I've already confirmed our flight."

Edgar Payne in the impresario tuxedo went and slowly sat down in the lounge chair in which he said he did his serious thinking and listening. (His wife had driven back to Long Island with the children immediately after the concert.)

Hattie remained standing. She held in her hand the check for the balance due her. Edgar Payne had given it to her the moment she returned from tucking Sonny in.

Midnight. It was close to midnight. Outside the living room windows, their shades drawn, Macon Street lay silent except for the occasional passing car or footsteps and, in the near-distance, the revved-up sound of Friday night, paycheck night, party night in the bucket-o'-blood bars and dance halls on Reid Avenue close by.

Edgar Payne sat for some time with his head bowed, listening it seemed to the revelry that rose and ebbed with each shift in the wind. When he finally raised up, his face with its carved, heavy features appeared calm, the slightly hooded eyes were as unyielding as always, and as he spoke the surface of his voice sounded equally calm.

"All right," he said. "All right. It seems I heard wrong. I was really hoping, though, that you'd be staying on a few days longer so Sonny could have a little more time with his cousins. But also so that the two of us would have a chance to talk about some things once the concert was out of the way. But that's not to be, so perhaps we could talk about them now . . ."

He hoped she wasn't too tired.

Not at all. And, yes, it would have to be now, because she would be busy packing all day tomorrow.

Hattie settled herself in the diva gown on the sofa directly across from his chair. She placed the check on the coffee table in front of her and waited, arms folded high on her chest in her characteristic pose, the winged sleeves of her gown hiding the loose flesh on her upper arms.

"It's about Sonny of course."

"I suspected as much."

"We need to do better by him, Hattie."

"And what exactly do you mean by that?"

"I'll tell you," he said, and legs crossed, the hand with

the great seal of a ring resting on his knee, all the light in the room gathered like a flock of birds on the shiny dome of his head, Edgar Payne proceeded to tell her, in precise undeniable detail, about their life, hers and Sonny's, on rue Sauffroy.

The two cramped rooms on the top floor with the communal toilet in the hall. And the building itself. He had been sent pictures of it. The gaping front door. The broken windows. The old, crumbling stone of the exterior. The clotheslines. He was in possession as well of pictures of the street and the neighborhood in general. It reminded him of Bed-Stuy at its worst.

This was where he had to walk to school, the boy, through dangerous streets such as these, and to a school that according to his information had one of the lowest ratings in the city.

"That's no place to raise him, Hattie. You know that. Not if it's possible to do better for him."

No response. Hattie unable to move or speak or even breathe.

As for the job she was so eager to return to. The Club Violette. It wasn't much of a job from what he had learned. And the kinds of things that went on there. No wonder it was always being closed down. He'd been given the facts on the place.

What was she doing at her age working in someplace little better than a strip joint?

And what was she thinking of—anger in his voice now—leaving the boy alone all night with an alcoholic old woman. Entrusting him to the care of someone like that!

"How . . . ?" Hattie finally found her voice, but it was barely audible and she could only manage the one word.

"How could I know so much? My dear Hattie, that's what lawyers are for. Especially those with colleagues and contacts overseas."

The man had given her his thin-lipped smile, had shaken her hand with a hand softer and smoother than any woman's, had asked her about the early spring weather in Paris. "Rain, I imagine," he'd said. And she had laughed and agreed, "What else? It's March."

"Bastards! You and your shyster lawyer! Bastards!"

"Careful," Edgar Payne said, motioning toward the corridor to the bedrooms. "We don't want to wake him."

"Digging around in my life! Hiring people to spy on me . . . ?"

He spread his hands. "You left us no choice. There was never a word from you about the boy. Yes, you wrote my mother when he was born to say you had custody, but that was it. Not a word from you after that. And no address for you. You made sure not to put it on the letter. No phone. For almost nine years you never so much as sent us a picture of him. Nothing. You simply disappeared off the face of the earth with my brother's grandson. As if you thought you owned him. No!" Anger again. "We couldn't allow that to go on. Something had to be done."

"Something had to be done . . ." Hattie slowly repeated and, slowly, overwhelmed, her gaze traveled around the room which was dominated by the large collection of Sonny-Rett records and CDs, searching for the understanding she needed somewhere there. Then, confronting him: "Something such as putting on a big concert in your brother's name, right, and inviting us? That's what you mean, isn't it? The whole thing a setup!" *Nothing's beyond that W.I.* Hadn't Florence Varina warned her? "And me like a fool fell for it!"

Edgar Payne, his own anger in check now, was noncommittal. "If that's the way you choose to see it, fine. All I'm concerned about, and you should be too, is what's best for Sonny. And you know, even if you won't admit it, that he'd have more of a chance here."

"I've got the papers!"

He dismissed them with a wave. "It's unlikely they'd hold up in court. I've already been told as much. Besides, I don't think you want to go that route. The courts, I mean. Not for yourself and certainly not for Sonny. Don't do that to him. My grandchildren still haven't recovered from the fighting over them that went on in court.

"Besides," he continued, "if you go that route, we'd have to get into even more of your business. Such as the way I've learned you, my brother, and Cherisse lived all those years. I personally don't care what went on with the three of you, what arrangement you all had, but it won't sound good in a court of law, even in France."

Hattie started to call him every name in the book only to be stopped by his raised hand and unrelenting voice.

"Another thing, we'd have to make an effort to find my niece. I'm sure the courts will want to know why a fourteen-year-old would suddenly run away from home and turn so wild—that's what you said in the letter to my mother. I know I do. I want to know. In fact, I'd like to try and find her, JoJo, my brother's child, and help her if I can. Alva and I talked about it after I drove you back to Brooklyn last Sunday. It's something else I planned to discuss with you once the concert was over. Sonny should at least know his mother."

"I have the papers!"

Voice sheering high. Edgar Payne patiently waited until the room recovered from its impact before speaking again.

"And there's another matter the courts will certainly be interested in—and I really didn't want to bring this up, but I see there's no reasoning with you.

"Your habit." He put it flatly. "The stuff, substances, whatever you call them we understand you obtain at that so-called nightclub."

A trapped and cornered look on Hattie's face.

Yes, that too, he said. The people they had hired had been thorough, expensive but thorough. She had left him no choice.

This time when she started to call him every name in the book he didn't stop her. The way she hurled them at him, the names—worse than any she had called Abe Kaiser the week before—could have been a barrage of stones in a Biblical stoning to the death.

When she had exhausted them all, Edgar Payne simply shrugged and said, "You remember what we used to say around the block when we were kids, don't you? 'Sticks and stones may break my bones but names will never harm me.' I'm used to them. You're not the only one who thinks the worst of me. I'm the Shylock of Central Brooklyn, remember?

"At any rate, let me make one thing clear. I mean to do right by the boy. And soon. I don't intend dragging this thing out. You say you're leaving on Sunday? All right. Let me know by tomorrow whether you'll be reasonable and we can work things out in the next few months or if we have to resort to the courts. But know that I'll be back and forth over there to see him until it's resolved."

He rose, visibly tired, his face haggard, although the suitor's pleated shirt and bow tie looked as fresh as if he had just put them on.

"Give him a chance, Hattie." Edgar Payne was suddenly

pleading. "He's the one hopeful thing that's come out of the thirty-year war and disunity on this block. Let him go. Over here will never be any paradise for us, we both know that, but at least I have the means to make things easier for him and to protect him as much as that's possible, something I should have done for my brother, had I the understanding at the time . . ."

He came to stand almost humbly in front of her, only the coffee table between them. "If you love him for himself, more than for something or someone you might be trying to hold on to through him, you'll give him a chance."

"What's that supposed to mean?" Hattie was on her feet.

"Give it some thought. I think you'll understand. And think about this too: Sometimes love—and I know how much you love him—is as much about letting go as it is about holding on."

Besides, she would be able to come visit him as often as she liked. He would see to that. And Sonny could spend summers with her.

And she would be provided for. He would see to that also. No more Club Violette. And a better place to live than rue Sauffroy.

"I don't need you to look after me!"

"My brother would have wanted it," he said and went on to explain how this would be arranged through the lawyer in Paris.

At the door, he stood for some time with his back to the room and his shoulders weighted down again with that thing, whatever it was, that remained unsaid.

Finally, head bowed: "He wrote to me once."

Hattie, who was still telling him, in no uncertain terms, that she didn't need him to support her, abruptly stopped.

"Who?"

"My brother. He wrote once asking me to take JoJo."

"What're you talking about?" Her voice fallen to a whisper again, she sank back down on the sofa.

"It was about a year before we heard he had died, when things must've been really going downhill for him. He asked me to take and raise her. But I never answered the letter. I was so angry at him for refusing to have any contact with us, and what that was doing to my mother, never mind she'd been wrong. We never even knew he had a child. And even though he wrote asking me to take her, he still didn't want us to know his whereabouts. There was no home address on the letter, just a post office box. Then at the time I was having my own troubles with my daughter who decided to drop out of college and get married . . .

"So I never wrote to him—my brother who died almost broke in the goddamn Paris subway, just how we really don't know. Talk about 'no hiding place down here,' as it says in the old spiritual—not for us at any rate. My brother sure found that out, didn't he? But who knows, maybe if I had answered his letter . . ."

He broke off, his face to the living room door with its formal, even austere Victorian paneling. He might have been confronting the harsh countenance of judgment.

"I don't understand. I don't understand . . ." Hattie repeating in numb disbelief to herself. "He wouldn't have done something like that. I raised her. She was my child! He wouldn't have just sent her away . . ."

"He was doing what he thought was best for her," Edgar

Payne said. He was still on the verge of leaving, his back to Hattie as well as to the room.

"And even if it had crossed his mind because he was feeling desperate, he would never have written to you or anybody else without telling me. No! Going behind my back? No!"

Edgar Payne looked almost sympathetically at her over his shoulder. "Well, it seems he didn't tell you everything. Which goes to show, I guess, how little we sometimes know—really know—even those closest to us . . .

"Anyway, I hope you can see why I've got to try and do right by the little fella inside. My brother would have wanted it."

He reached for the doorknob.

Hattie. Her voice raised. At first, caught between sleep and wake, he thought he was back home in his own bed, listening to her berating Madame Molineaux again for not doing her job. She had come in from work to find his *nounou* dead asleep in her apartment and the alarm clock that was to alert her to look in on him every two hours ringing unheeded. It happened from time to time. Too much Père Magloire, and Hattie was letting her have it but good.

Except that she was speaking English. So was the voice opposing hers, which was nowhere as loud. And it was a man's voice.

His uncle and Hattie quarreling? How come? Hadn't they just been all smiles at the concert? Hadn't his uncle planted a big, happy kiss on Hattie's cheek onstage to thank her for the stories about his grandfather? Hadn't they toasted and congratulated each other at the reception afterward on how well everything had gone? And now the two of them quarreling? Their angry back-and-forth voices reaching all the way into his sleep. What could they be quarreling about? Quickly he drew the bedcovers over his head. He didn't want to know. He didn't want to hear the actual words. And he didn't want to go nowhere near them. Because whose side would he take, loving them both as he did? Big People. There was no understanding them.

He waited, hunkered under the covers, his arms tight across his chest to keep the balloon inside from filling up and cutting off his breathing, one hand reaching down to hold his *zizi*, although this time that offered him no comfort. Until, finally, he heard the footsteps he waited for each day going heavily down the stairs. His uncle Edgar leaving. He'd be back to see him tomorrow, though, *and the day after tomorrow and the day after day after day after that forever.*

Of that he was certain.

When the last footstep died, he slipped out of bed and crept up the corridor toward the front room, the hardwood floor cold under his feet after the warmth of the covers. Picking his way through the shards of the two-week visit.

Hattie on the sofa didn't look his way as he entered the living room, nor did she acknowledge his presence when he came and sat beside her. She was staring across at the empty lounge chair, her face drained and unreadable under the turban with the closed-locket brooch at its center.

He didn't think it wise to ask just yet what was wrong, why the quarrel with his uncle, instead he quietly slipped his hand into hers, as he always did when she was upset and hadn't taken her *médicaments*, to soothe her and to restore her to herself as well as to him.

For the first time that he could remember, nothing happened. She didn't suddenly rally with apologies and hugs. No spanking herself on the hand to make him laugh. Indeed, the hand he held remained slack and unresponsive. A stranger's hand.

Silence, except for the sound of her unsettled breathing.

He saw the check on the coffee table and, curious, leaned forward to see how much it was for. But since it was in dollars which he didn't know how to convert into francs he couldn't tell how much the zeros he saw represented.

"Money! Money'll do it every time!" A sudden outburst, then silence again.

She had repeatedly threatened to tear up the check his uncle had sent her in the mail and toss the pieces like so much trash into the Seine, only to change her mind and spend every penny of it on him.

"No need for you to go there looking like a pauper," she'd said.

A moonless night outside the living room windows. In a few hours the drawn shades would gradually turn a pale spring yellow, morning arriving, another day unfolding, and with it would come the usual sounds of life on Macon Street: people and cars and the chorusing of hammers up and down the block—that is, if the men his uncle hired worked on Saturdays. Black men in hard hats a brighter yellow than the sun, working. He had searched for the lowly *vendeur* among them.

Finally a sidelong glance his way, although it did not include his face. "Where's your bathrobe? Where're your slippers?"

Hattie sounding angry with him too. Quickly he ran and put them on. Like everything else they were new.

Another glance when he returned, to see that he had done as he'd been told. But again the glance bypassed his face. Hattie, who had been fathermothersisterbrother and all other kin until now, was for some reason deliberately avoiding the sight of his face.